YUBA ISUKARI

Illustration by
Tatsuyuki Tanaka

YOKOHAMA STATION SF NATIONAL

Yuba Isukari

Translation by Stephen Paul
Cover art by Tatsuyuki Tanaka

YOKOHAMA EKI SF ZENKOKUBAN
©Yuba Isukari, Tatsuyuki Tanaka 2017
First published in Japan in 2017 by KADOKAWA CORPORATION, Tokyo.
English translation rights arranged with KADOKAWA CORPORATION, Tokyo through
TUTTLE-MORI AGENCY, INC., Tokyo.

English translation © 2022 by Yen Press, LLC

Yen On
150 West 30th Street, 19th Floor
New York, NY 10001

Visit us at yenpress.com ❖ facebook.com/yenpress ❖ twitter.com/yenpress
yenpress.tumblr.com ❖ instagram.com/yenpress

First Yen On Edition: June 2022
Edited by Yen On Editorial: Jordan Blanco
Designed by Yen Press Design: Wendy Chan

Yen On is an imprint of Yen Press, LLC.
The Yen On name and logo are trademarks of Yen Press, LLC.

Library of Congress Cataloging-in-Publication Data
Names: Isukari, Yuba, author. | Tanaka, Tatsuyuki, illustrator. | Paul, Stephen (Translator), translator.
Title: Yokohama Station SF national / Yuba Isukari ; illustration by Tatsuyuki Tanaka ;
    translation by Stephen Paul.
Other titles: Yokohama Station SF zenkokuban. English
Description: First Yen On edition. | New York : Yen On, 2022.
Identifiers: LCCN 2022010534 | ISBN 9781975344177 (hardcover)
Subjects: CYAC: Science fiction. | Short stories. | LCGFT: Science fiction. | Short stories.
Classification: LCC PZ7.1.I896 Yok 2022 | DDC [Fic]—dc23
LC record available at https://lccn.loc.gov/2022010534

ISBNs: 978-1-9753-4417-7 (paperback)
       978-1-9753-4418-4 (ebook)

10 9 8 7 6 5 4 3 2 1

LSC-C

Printed in the United States of America

CONTENTS :::

YUBA ISUKARI PRESENTS

YOKOHAMA
STATION SF
NATIONAL

PROLOGUE

December 197 (Station Year), Matsumae Peninsula, Hokkaido

Under a layer of clouds so thick it was impossible to tell if the sun had gone down or not, the snow was falling heavily enough to impede one's vision. A layer of white covered the treeless landscape. The narrow strip of land featured several shipping container-like buildings, behind which was a small mountain, its slope ablaze with a yellow glow.

The lights were attached to wooden scaffolding that rested against the slope, and on the interior side of the frame was a small tunnel mouth, steel beams jutting around it like the ribs of some massive creature. From a distance, it looked like a construction site at night. More accurately, however, this was a location for the *prevention* of construction.

Above the tunnel was affixed a metal plate that read SEIKAN TUNNEL. It was JR North Japan's ultimate line of defense against Yokohama Station's invasion into Hokkaido.

Fifty years had already passed since the self-replicating Yokohama Station covered the island of Honshu entirely. The Tsugaru Strait was too wide for the station's structure to cross, so the only thing that needed to be done to prevent it from reaching Hokkaido was to seal off the exit of the Seikan Tunnel. Compared to the southern front that Kyushu was fighting at the Kanmon Straits, this was much easier.

Once suitably doused in the yellow light, the steel beams sticking out of the tunnel entrance could be cut into pieces, then loaded on trucks and taken somewhere else. The metal being replicated by Yokohama Station, once sufficiently de-Yokohama Stationized, was melted down and reused.

"It's a shame that for all the material we're receiving this way, that wooden scaffolding has to cheapen the whole look of it," lamented a young employee wearing a thick work uniform. The foreman's metal container housing kept out the snow and wind. However, it possessed little in the way of insulation, and only the wood-burning stove could keep away the winter chill that constantly seeped inside.

"It's to protect against contamination," said the middle-aged foreman. He had a neat little mustache and wore a coat that resembled a Russian army one from back in the days of the Gregorian calendar. "Organic material is much harder for Yokohama Station's structure to contaminate than metal and concrete. What would be the point of setting up a scaffold to stop the station from expanding if it's the first thing that gets absorbed by the station?"

"Couldn't you just shine the canceler at the scaffolding, too?"

"At the whole massive structure? It'd be a waste of power," replied the foreman, fiddling with his facial hair.

There were many of the enormous yellow lamps, which looked like theater spotlights, installed around the structure. Fat cables transmitting energy ran from the devices into the tunnel. Strange as it was, the electricity used to prevent Yokohama Station's invasion was being taken from Yokohama Station itself.

Lines ran across the screen of an oscilloscope sitting on the desk of the container building.

"Sir, we have a number of feral turnstiles approaching. Distance of fifty meters. They'll be on the camera any moment now. Ah, there they are," said the young employee just as the automated turnstiles appeared on the display in front of the foreman. They had flat, boardlike bodies and limbs that extended from them like table legs. The head displays, which looked unnaturally tacked-on, wore frozen smiles.

"Turn off the cancelers," instructed the foreman. The yellow lights attached to the wooden scaffolding went out, and the site below the heavy clouds became even darker.

"Three...no, four of them. Shall we destroy them?"

"Don't bother—no need to use valuable weaponry. The turnstiles don't come out of the station anyway. Leave them be, and they'll turn back around before long," the foreman stated. No sooner had he done so than the bell sounded to indicate the end of the regular work shift. The younger employee gave a huge yawn, opened the door, and pulled out some beer that had been stuck into the snow outside.

"Shall we celebrate the end of the day with a drink, sir?" he proposed, bringing the white cans inside. The foreman could have told him off, instructed him to go back to the barracks, but his workplace responsibility had vanished with the chime, and instead, he only spoke of primitive desires.

"I'd prefer hot sake instead."

"Hey, all alcohol will warm you up if you give it time. And this was a gift from the Hakodate folks," the young man remarked, handing one can to his superior. He waited for him to pull the tab before cracking open his own. "Being the Defense Bureau and all, I thought we'd be having shoot-outs with the turnstiles, but it's rare even to see them here. Nothing but grinding down the endlessly growing building, huh?"

"That's right. Normally, the turnstiles keep much farther back into the tunnel."

"Aren't they supposed to be the station guards?"

"They're the *Inside* guards, technically. There are places in Yokohama Station where you need a Suika and places where you don't. The automated turnstiles police those boundaries. And that's much deeper in the tunnel."

"Ohhh. So the interior of the station and Inside are different things? That's hard to follow."

"You get used to it."

"Do people ever come out? I mean, people from Honshu with Suika credentials are allowed to go outside, right?"

"You think someone's going to walk all the way through the Seikan Tunnel? What do Inside folk want with this barren land?"

"Huh. I like it, though."

The foreman snorted with laughter.

"...By the way, if you'll excuse the elementary question," the junior of the two began. "Why do we turn off the structural genetic field cancelers when the turnstiles come? Is it bad if they get into the light?"

"No. It has no direct effect on them... Do you know how the canceler works?"

"Yes. You're shining a localized antiphase field back, right? That eliminates the structural genetic field, meaning the corresponding material is no longer Yokohama Station, and it loses the ability to replicate," answered the young man, quoting the knowledge he was taught after joining the company. The actual mechanisms of Yokohama Station's growth were kept secret from the general populace of Hokkaido, so new JR employees had to learn the fundamentals in their first year.

"Right. Automated turnstiles can distinguish Yokohama Station from everything else. They will not venture into a space where the canceler has been deployed. However, if you shine the canceler where they are, it creates a situation where automated turnstiles are present *where the station isn't*. And that's when it causes problems."

"Problems?"

"I've only seen it happen a few times, myself. That head just falls right off. They put their hands on the floor and go quadrupedal."

"And then what happens?"

"They attack people."

There was a heavy silence for a moment.

"With guns."

"What? Those things have guns? I thought they only had wires for apprehending trespassers."

"Look, see that hole?" the foreman said, pointing at the wall of the container house. There was a glob of earth-colored resin stuck to the metal surface. It seemed to be patching up a hole.

"The weapons aren't very big compared to their body size, so you can deal with them if you stay calm and focused, but you always want to minimize casualties, see."

"So basically, if they're put into a state their programming doesn't allow for, they go crazy?"

"Perhaps."

The young man tried to imagine the sight of an automated turnstile crawling around on all fours. The limbs were all about the same length, so dropping down would put the body at a level angle, just like a table. That almost made it seem like the limbs were designed for quadrupedal movement all along. Supposedly, human arms shrank to be much shorter after thousands upon thousands of generations walking on two legs.

"By the way, is Miss Rube on vacation? I haven't seen her today."

"Rube was transferred to headquarters in Sapporo."

"What? I thought she'd be so happy to have some real beer for once. Though I guess they must have plenty at HQ. What division?"

"Engineering 2nd Division. They've had a lot of resignations lately. They were starving for new blood."

"...The infamous 2nd Division, huh?" The younger man appeared almost reverential. "That's where they have the saboteur android agents we send Inside. I was stunned when I learned we had the tech to do that."

"It's no surprise you were unaware. Such things didn't even exist until ten years ago." The foreman took a swig of beer. "That was around the time of that scandal, remember? They replaced a whole batch of principal officials in the company. Everything changed after that. Same thing with the canceler. In fact, the whole reason we've been able to repel the station so effectively..."

He trailed off, suddenly becoming pensive, anxious.

They'd pushed the front line of Yokohama Station's advance from Hokkaido back to the Seikan Tunnel. For JR North Japan—and all the people of Hokkaido—that was something worth celebrating wholeheartedly. Yet the foreman's voice was heavy. It seemed to suggest they were under the rule of some dangerous, misunderstood power they weren't meant to have.

YOKOHAMA
STATION SF
NATIONAL

Seto Inland Sea & Kyoto

A Harsh Mistress

1

June 198 (Station Year), Okayama, Northeast of Great Seto Bridge

Violent rain lashed at the concrete surface, with its equally turbulent undulations, signaling the arrival of the wet season. Clouds utterly blocked out the moonlight so that only the glow from Inside illuminated the ground. Yokohama Station covered Honshu, but the Okayama region was close to the western edge, and its structures had only recently been generated. The floor was formed of unspecialized concrete, its structural purpose not yet fixed.

In places where many people came and went, like the cities of Kofu and Matsumoto, such spaces like this one inevitably became hallways that piled up and overlapped until they took the shape of a multilevel city. But in lowly populated areas like these, only a bare minimum of corridors appeared, and the rest remained untended concrete with the texture of soapy water.

Here and there in Yokohama Station were doors that allowed access to the roof from Inside, but few citizens ever ventured through them, especially during monsoon and typhoon season. The toxic rain clouds from the Winter War era were clean now, as two centuries had passed. However, most people Inside were ignorant of that fact. To them, rain would always inspire fear.

So if anything was moving about on the roof during a storm, it couldn't be human. Yet it was not an automated turnstile, either. It was a Corpocker-3 android, made with the finest engineering in all of JR North Japan, and it bore the appearance of a young girl.

"Haikunterke, can you hear me?"

The voice from Suikanet entered her primary memory device. It was the voice of Kaeriyama, a technical officer of JR North Japan.

"There's no place around you where you might be able to block out the net. I was hoping for some exposed natural hillside, but oh well. Head out to sea instead."

"Roger that," replied Haikunterke, calling up a map from her supplemental memory device. It was a straight twenty-five-kilometer shot to the Seto Inland Sea. Confirming that she had adequate power reserves, she began to run to the south. Despite the extreme fluctuations in the concrete surface, several meters at times, her specially designed body proved capable of traversing it as easily as if running on flat ground.

She reached the seaside in about an hour. There was a strip of exposed natural ground between the station and the shoreline, a buffer several dozen meters wide. A long line of pine trees grew there, most likely the descendants of trees people had planted to preserve the sand line.

"It's Haikunterke. I've just reached the coast."

"All right. Cross the water and head to Shikoku. I was planning on using the Great Seto Bridge, but it looks like we don't have the time for that. Based on the turnstile movements, its immune memory is quite strong around there. You should get away from the Inside."

Kaeriyama's voice held a nuance of unease and resignation. She guessed he was probably against sending her over the water rather than the bridge but had been overruled.

"I'll do that. But I won't be able to access the net for a while."

"…I know. There should be increasing Stationization in the Kagawa area, but we don't have any accurate information about the net status there. Find a way to contact us as soon as you can. Good luck."

"I'll do my best."

Haikunterke ended the connection there. She cut down some nearby pine trees and spread out a water-resistant plastic sheet she'd acquired

Inside to make a simple raft with a canopy. She'd heard that android bodies were waterproof already, but she didn't want to take any unnecessary risks in the sea.

She checked her power level. It was adequate for now, but there was no telling when she'd be able to recharge again. Best to let the waves carry her and minimize the energy usage. She rowed the raft out into the water.

The Seto Inland Sea was inky black. After a while, she finally reached a place with no Suikanet signal. That should finally put an end to the immune response, and Haikunterke breathed a sigh of relief. It also meant there was no determining her precise location, however.

The automated turnstiles of Yokohama Station purged anything moving that was not an element of the station. Many exceptions existed, however, including humans with a Suika implant and children under the age of six. The reason JR North Japan's android saboteurs looked like human children was to take advantage of this quirk of the station's immune system.

Unfortunately, once they were active Inside for long enough, the station's defenses began to learn and identified them as a threat for the turnstiles to eliminate. Since reaching the Noto Peninsula on the north side of Honshu, Haikunterke had been within the Suikanet's range for several months consecutively, allowing it to develop an immune response for her. She needed to distance herself until the net could no longer identify her and let its memory of her fade over time.

A faint light was visible in the direction the raft was drifting. It looked like part of Yokohama Station, but it could also have been the glow of civilization on the small islands within the Seto Inland Sea. Haikunterke couldn't detect the net waves continuously emitted from the station structure, but the light seemed a little too large to be coming from a human construction.

Ultimately, it was neither of those things.

It turned out to be a structure that looked alien, even from a distance. It resembled a building, except that it possessed no straight beams or walls. The entire edifice was bent and curved at odd angles.

The windowpanes were similarly twisted into rhombus shapes, allowing dim light to spill through. It was like Yokohama Station had fallen unconscious in mid-stretch or like a melting gingerbread house.

"A station spore," Haikunterke muttered. "I've never actually seen one before."

It was a piece of Yokohama Station that had landed on this remote island through some means, then built itself up entirely on its own. The structural genetic field was incomplete and could not create a proper building, and its growth capability was extremely weak compared to the main body of Yokohama Station.

There were many possible causes for the scattering, from the movement of ships contaminated with the structural genetic field to drifting materials. The phenomenon only occurred in rare cases on tiny islands that were the proper distance from the mainland. JR North Japan was only aware of a handful of such cases.

Because it was not in physical contact with Yokohama Station, there was no danger of Suikanet sending its immune memory here. Even better, it seemed there was power in the spore. Haikunterke decided to land on the island.

At a closer distance, she could see that the station spore covered the western half of the small island, which measured about two kilometers across. The eastern side was natural ground with jutting terrain and thick tree growth. Haikunterke brought the raft to shore there and pulled it onto the sand so it would not drift away.

The android climbed up a hill to get a view of the area. It wasn't very open, but it was enough for her to tell that there was no light source aside from the spore itself. Still, out of an abundance of caution, she increased the sensitivity of her auditory and visual systems.

Then she walked around the vicinity of the strange building, collecting observational data. A station spore was a precious source of information when it came to understanding the nature of Yokohama Station—so much so that there had been plans to grow one on a remote island near Hokkaido for research purposes. The idea was only rejected due to the risks it posed.

"No matter furnace signals. Unclear if the isolated structural genetic field is missing the information for a matter furnace or if the size is too small to generate one. The energy source is most likely rooftop photo-absorption panels. Based on the degree of genetic field mutation, I estimate this spore's age at nearly a hundred years. Its energy supply density is low in comparison to the real thing and so slow to develop that it still hasn't covered this little island in all that time..."

She sent this comment to her supplemental memory device as an attachment to her observational data. Because all of her information was likely to be sent in one batch at some point in the future, the comments were a necessary context to keep headquarters back in Sapporo from being overwhelmed and confused.

JR North Japan, perpetually scarce on resources, had gone through painful measures to produce this special android body. Haikunterke still did not agree that she should have been given such a valuable thing. She had always thought it should be Samayunkur's.

Back when they were still connected with cables and could easily share their thoughts with each other, his excellence had stood out. He accurately judged a matter by the smallest of informational input, and his ability to retain details from the same data as everyone else was clearly superior. Samayunkur understood what they were before they were taught, which came as a shock to the technicians.

He should've been the one to receive this special body and take on the mission to travel to the very ends of Yokohama Station. That was what all sixteen of them—or at least, the fifteen aside from him—must have thought.

However, it was Haikunterke's main memory device loaded into this particular android body. She knew her results were middling and did not understand why she had been chosen. After demanding the answer from her technician, Kaeriyama, he had only said that it was on Yukie's orders. "Trust in her, and trust in me," he'd told her.

One week before her departure, Haikunterke had still been unused to the high-functioning body, and she was walking around the facility with clumsy steps when a boy in a standard form came to see her.

"Hi, is that you, Terke? It's me, Samayunkur," he greeted, smiling.

It was a very natural expression, just like an actual human's. Haikunterke was bad at such subtle displays. She had practiced raising the angle of the ends of her mouth in front of the mirror many times, but it always looked unnatural, as if she had taken a photograph of her face and was forcing it out of shape. Even now, after nearly two years on her mission in Yokohama Station, she hardly ever used her facial appearance capabilities. It just wasn't necessary.

"I've been assigned to the Tohoku region, along with Yaieyukar. We're leaving in two months," Samayunkur said. That was the region closest to Hokkaido, with the least urgency and danger involved. She had assumed that Nepshamai would be picked for that one.

"Ah. I'm going to Shikoku," Haikunterke replied. She still wasn't quite used to moving her mouth as she spoke.

"I know. You're leaving next week, aren't you?" he questioned. Haikunterke wondered if he had come to complain to her that she had received the prestige of this exclusive body and critical mission instead of him.

Contrary to her expectations, he did not seem upset in the slightest. "What do you think will happen to the four who didn't receive any bodies?" he asked. "Do you think they'll just be on standby until they get orders?"

Haikunterke knew that was unlikely to pass. While Samayunkur had excelled under the same education the rest of the group received, others stood out for their poor performance. Compared with a body that required significant amounts of rare metals, a primary memory device demanded plenty of time to produce, but at a more reasonable cost. Those in charge had to be working on their next robots already. The four who were left over would probably never be used. Thus, Haikunterke said nothing.

Samayunkur shrugged and said, "It's too bad we won't see each other for so long, Terke, especially now that we've got bodies to use. Are you nervous about the mission?"

"I am. I might make a mistake that will ruin this expensive form. I might fail to fulfill my objectives and die all alone Inside."

Afterward, someone might state, *"We should've sent Samayunkur."* Haikunterke agreed, but she couldn't bring herself to admit it aloud.

Inside missions were dangerous. The previous generation, the

Corpocker-2s, were not nearly as humanlike because of technical reasons. They more closely resembled the automated turnstiles. Their onboard intelligence was low, so they were primarily controlled remotely using Suikanet. All of them were gone within a year of their mission. A few were eliminated by the turnstiles when the station's immune response kicked in. Others were destroyed by Insiders who recognized the machines as fakes. More still simply broke down and were unretrievable.

The next group to be produced was the third generation, including Haikunterke. Their resemblance to humans meant there was virtually no fear of being destroyed by Inside residents. Plus, it was much harder for the station to develop a way to recognize them for what they were. It did not mean there was no peril at all, however.

"Yes, we might even die. What do you think happens to us when we perish?" asked Samayunkur.

"They can replicate us," Haikunterke answered, stone-faced.

"Not perfectly. We're not just digital data, strictly speaking. No matter what, a copy is going to be inferior."

"That's only a technical problem, not a real one. We are only one for now, but we can be two or three. And we can be zero. It's as simple as that, in my opinion."

"Your sound is lagging. You have to speak in sync with your mouth movements," Samayunkur said, grinning and pointing at his own cheek. "Well, anyway, I suppose there's no life after death for us."

"Not for humans, either."

"You think not?"

"Do you believe there is, Kur?"

"Nope." He laughed.

Nearly two years had passed since their Inside mission commenced. Kaeriyama would send Haikunterke a general outline of the progress of her fellows' missions, but for some reason, he would always cleverly avoid giving details when it came to Samayunkur. She didn't even know if he was still active in the Tohoku region or if he had been recalled to headquarters. There was no communicating with other agents directly through Suikanet. It was technically possible, but the androids weren't given the module to make it happen.

"Why do you suppose they don't let us talk to each other? Do you think Yukie's afraid we're going to band together Inside and rebel against her?" Samayunkur had asked Haikunterke before they'd left home. "Do you want to start a revolution?" she questioned, but he just laughed it off.

"Not at all. But if I were going to fight back against headquarters, I would probably want your help, Terke. You'd be the most powerful one of us."

"So you just want me for my body," Haikunterke responded. Samayunkur looked at her with surprise for a moment, then burst into chuckles.

Most of her conversations with him happened before either had been hooked up to their supplemental memory devices, so they weren't saved as audio records. She couldn't go back and consult the logs word for word. However, Haikunterke still retained the things they talked about as impressions. She assumed that this was similar to how human memories worked.

"…Mimi?"

The voice took her by surprise. She turned around to see that someone had appeared from the woods behind the station spore. The android had been so preoccupied with her observation that she'd stopped paying attention to her surroundings.

It was a man she might have mistaken for a wild bear. He was large, sported a thick beard, and wore pelts. Of course, there was no way to get real animal pelts on the Japanese archipelago anymore. It was water-resistant fake fur manufactured in the Kansai region of Yokohama Station. He seemed to be around forty years old.

"There you are, Mimi. What are you doing here?" the man said. His voice was strangely high-pitched for someone who looked like a beast. He approached Haikunterke with odd, weak steps. He was squinting at her, too; perhaps his eyesight was poor.

"Who are you?" Haikunterke shouted. The rain made it hard to project her voice.

"Mimi? Wait…you're not? Oh. You aren't. Of course you aren't…," he replied before sighing heavily. "I'm sorry. You look like someone I used to know."

He bowed his head in apology.

2

"I'm Shido. Shido Kumano. I live on this island." The wild-looking man introduced himself in a high-pitched voice that didn't match his size. "Who are you? Where did you come from?"

Haikunterke checked and confirmed that Shido was not emitting any signature Suika brain waves on a sudden whim.

"...Haikunterke."

"That's a strange name. You from Shikoku?"

She tried to bob her head in a way that might be construed as a nod. At the very least, this suggested that the man did not interact with anyone from the island of Shikoku. Most likely, he was from the Inside. Yet if Haikunterke couldn't detect any traces of Suika on him, that meant he hadn't been in Yokohama Station for quite a long time. He'd probably been exiled from the station for Suika violation.

"You crossed the sea on that boat? Were you on the run?" the man inquired, pointing at the raft on the shore. Haikunterke nodded again. Until she knew more about this man's background, she did not want to give away any information. Such judgment calls were one area where significant variation existed among the saboteur agents. Nepshamai, in the Kanto region, was the kind to talk about all sorts of things he thought necessary to say, even if they weren't asked of him.

"I guess things must still be really bad in Shikoku. I've been living on this island a long time, but I'm too scared to go near there."

"Are there others here?"

"Nope. Been alone here for years, and you're the first to show up. It's a long journey from Shikoku, so they've never made the trip. There are a couple of folks around Shodoshima and Teshima, I think. But I suppose they're afraid of this island. On account of that strange building."

Based on the names of the islands Shido mentioned and the map data in her supplemental memory, Haikunterke had a relatively good idea of her current location. She was right in the middle of the Seto Inland Sea between Honshu and Shikoku. It was the perfect place to avoid Suikanet's coverage and wait out its immune memory.

The man hoisted up the large bag he had placed on the ground and said, "Well, why don't you come in and get out of the rain?"

Shido Kumano walked off, and Haikunterke followed him in silence. She would need to stay here for a while to investigate the spore. As such, it suited her purposes to know just who this man was.

Shido's home was atop a hill with a good view of the island's south side. It was a container house, the sort popular during the Winter War. As the name suggested, it was a metal box with the bare minimum of living materials within. These homes had been mass-produced when the attacks on cities were frequent and fierce, so that you could pull one with a truck and flee for safety at a moment's notice. Many of the homes in Hokkaido were containers, and Haikunterke had heard that in east Hokkaido, there were nomads who roamed around in them, gathering relics of the pre-war era.

Shido's home had not been moved in a long time, however. Thick roots twined around the satellite TV antenna, which hadn't received any signal in many decades. It likely hadn't been his house initially, just a leftover structure that had belonged to some different resident of the island long ago.

Once he got to the little building, he opened up a poly bag and asked, "You hungry? Here, have this," handing her a piece of bread. It was a roll about twenty centimeters long and torn off on both ends, for some reason. Haikunterke took the food, put it into her mouth, and chewed. Her body could not digest organic material, but she thought it wise to act like a human for now.

Shido pulled quite a large number of torn-off rolls from the bag, stuffed most of them into a cupboard, and ate one for himself.

"You want something to drink? I've got filtered rainwater."

"I'm fine," Haikunterke replied. "Why do you live here?"

"I went on the run, too. From Inside, in my case. You know Inside? It's the big island to the north," he explained. Shido was evidently having difficulty figuring out where to begin his story, probably because he believed he was talking to a six-year-old. Haikunterke felt it was best to play the part, but she didn't know how a six-year-old girl was supposed to act. There were no memories to that effect in her main memory device.

"I did some stuff Inside, and the important people there kicked me out."

"You did something bad? Did you break stuff?"

"No, it wasn't bad. But I made the important Inside people angry. So I ran away from them."

"What do you mean, important people?"

"They're called turnstiles. They're very, very scary."

"Oh."

"Don't you have anywhere else to go? If not, you can stay here. There's plenty of water and food, so I don't have any problem with another person being around."

Shido Kumano smiled kindly at her.

Present situation: Landed on island in Seto Inland Sea. Half covered by station spore (attached image 1). Outside of network range, so precise location is unclear, but likely around here (coordinates 1). One resident. Shido Kumano, male, exile from Inside. Age around 40, background unknown (attached image 2). Will stay on island for some time to gather information about spore. Haikunterke.

Haikunterke compressed the brief message and stored it in her communications module. Once she reached a place with any amount of Suikanet signal, it would automatically send the data to JR North Japan. That was going to be quite a long time in the future, however. There was no reception anywhere she went on the island, and the weather was too poor to go out into the water again. Given her objective of waiting out the immune memory, that suited her just fine.

Haikunterke continued collecting data about the station spore. Thanks to its flawed structural genetic field, the building resembled avant-garde artwork. Still, like the real Yokohama Station, it did end-lessly produce and expel a variety of matter on the inside.

However, the spore's products were warped, much like the building itself. The torn-off pieces of bread Shido always gave her were bits he'd pulled off of what the spore created, which were single bread rolls that measured dozens of meters long. But at least they knew what kind of food it was. Others were white blocks of condensed protein and hunks of vitamin-carrying fiber. Shido called them "eggs" and "veggies" and ate them without pause. If Haikunterke were a biological human, she would not want to eat them. There was also a pipe that produced a dark green sludge. When passed through a tank connected to the container house, it became fuel that powered the little building. The spore had a circumference of several kilometers, and it seemed like Shido knew precisely where everything within that range could be found.

While Haikunterke studied the nature of the station spore, she helped Shido with his daily tasks. Despite looking like a hardy wild animal, the man was actually in poor health. He spent one day out of every three sleeping and helpless in his home. He said that her arrival had made things much easier for him, but he also seemed guilty about having a small child doing hard work for him.

Haikunterke wanted to search inside the spore, too, but the struc-tural genetic field canceler worked poorly here, and it wasn't easy to open a hole she could use to get inside. The waveform of the genetic field was too different from the proper Yokohama Station on the main-land. Modifying the canceler to overwrite this altered waveform data was possible (the workings of the device were saved in her supplemen-tal memory), but it risked destroying the tool. Tinkering with mecha-nisms wasn't Haikunterke's strongest suit. *Samayunkur would probably do well at it*, she thought. In fact, she learned sometime later that the reason he was able to act like such a natural human being was that he had modified his own android body to do so.

At night, Haikunterke listened to Shido's stories. The android hardly ever spoke to him about herself, but the man didn't seem to mind. "You've had it hard," he would say. "You don't have to speak about it until you want to. You've been a big help to me just by being here."

It seemed to her that he believed she was a little girl with deep mental scars who had escaped Shikoku after a harrowing experience.

It had been a very long time since Haikunterke had followed a twenty-four-hour cycle. Inside, such a thing held almost no meaning. She needed sleep to recompile and store her memories, but she'd done so only when necessary and when there was a safe place for it.

After several days, Shido finally realized that Haikunterke was much too smart to be a five- or six-year-old girl and began to speak in more specific terms about himself. One day, he described his past.

"Inside, I lived in a city called Kyoto. I was a member of the Dodger Alliance."

"Dodger Alliance?"

"Never heard of it, huh? We were pretty famous Inside."

Haikunterke quickly shook her head. It was a name in JR North Japan's list of Inside groups to be wary of, but someone from Shikoku couldn't have possibly known that, and so it was imperative that she acted as though she didn't, either.

"I get that you were in that group...but why were you kicked out of Inside?"

"You want to know? It's a very long story."

Haikunterke bobbed her head, just a little bit.

"I've never told this to anyone else. I mean, I haven't had anyone to tell it to," Shido began, laughing.

3

Shido Kumano was born in a small village Inside, on the southern part of the Kii Peninsula, which stretched down west of Shikoku. *Village* was probably the right word for a settlement of that size. It had almost no hallways connecting it to the bigger cities, and the guide maps were inaccurate because the paths were complex and mazelike. Unsurprisingly, visitors were rare.

The village was a five-level area formed on the side of a mountain. Because its population was so small, the station structure did not grow larger for them. It had maintained the same multilevel system since Shido's grandfather's generation.

The Kumano family lived on the third floor. They were bioelectric technicians and had been for generations. Their job was implanting Suikas into the village children, as well as performing the Suikanet registration process for them. The net demanded a registration cost of 500,000 milliyen, and Shido's family charged their own personal fee on top. They would use this money to buy food made on the first level and industrial goods from the second floor.

A short distance from the village was a food production factory. They planted and grew rice and vegetables in a giant open space under huge red lights. This type of facility required human labor to function, and by village law, only those who lived on the first level could work there. Residents of the second level could collect food, electronics, and fuel that popped out of the station here and there, and they performed simple tasks like assembling machines. They consumed part of their findings and sold the rest to higher floors.

For people on the first level, the 500,000 milliyen needed to acquire a Suika was more or less equivalent to a lifetime of earnings, so money's sole purpose to them was to give their children Suika access. In other words, the people who were born on the first level needed to spend their entire lives working for the right to exist in Yokohama Station. The children of laborers who could no longer pay the cost were taken by the automated turnstiles and dumped somewhere else. Consequently, the population level stayed almost entirely flat.

In most cities, people of greater social status tended to live on higher floors as a general trend, but it was written into law in this village. Each family had its profession, and every profession had its own strata. Those born on the third level had a particular status unique to them and would always. It had ever been that way.

Third-floorers like Shido's family were the technical experts compared to the simple workers of the lower levels. In addition to bioelectric engineering, they performed Suikanet maintenance and gave orders to the laborers.

Villagers on the fourth floor performed administrative tasks that kept the settlement running, while the fifth level was exclusively for the ruling family. Every now and then, those from higher floors came down to present some new regulations, purchase supplies from the residents, then leave. There was no tax system in the village, so nobody knew how their sovereigns came by the milliyen they paid to the lower people for their goods.

It was a remarkably stable class system. The village was relatively isolated from everything else, so no one had any misgivings about the way it all worked. They didn't even have a policing force as the cities did.

When Shido was young, there was one resident from the first floor who couldn't take it anymore and struck a visiting fourth-floorer with a stick. The automated turnstiles appeared in no time and took that man away. He never returned.

Because the turnstiles forbade all violence Inside, the lower classes did not stage aggressive uprisings despite the advantage of numbers. The only kind of resistance they could manage was running away.

Shido had few complaints about life on the third floor. He was afforded ample necessities and enough spending money to buy luxuries from the occasional traveling merchant. Work time was short. Children on the third floor had a little compulsory education and technical training. However, once it was done, the rest of Shido's childhood was mostly spent reading materials he acquired from Suikanet. Most of them were novels that detailed the lives of anonymous people who lived in the biggest cities, like Kofu and Matsumoto. He would read them and dream of one day visiting those places, but it was only ever a furtive desire that he could not act upon.

He was betrothed to a longtime friend, a girl named Mimi. Not because they were in love but because their families were not too closely related, they were near in age, and there were almost no other available women on the third floor. The matter had been arranged as a matter of course not long after they were born. Shido had assumed at a young age that he would live his entire life in the village. That he would one day be exiled from all of Yokohama Station was inconceivable.

An odd man came to the village when Shido was twenty. He made his way through the labyrinth of the mountain passages and approached the residents of the first floor, exclaiming with excitement as though discovering some rare species of animal. "Well, well, I didn't expect to find a settlement out here! This is a huge discovery! What a fantastic find!"

The villagers, however, were alarmed. On occasion, traders made their way over, usually carrying large cargo boxes or pulling carts. Yet rather than having a vehicle, this man was leading a number of automated turnstiles. Old ropes were tied around their slender arms, and they followed the orders that he gave them from a handheld device in his possession.

One villager began to worship him. "The god of Yokohama Station has come to us as a man!" Others hid their children, thinking the stranger was a wicked conjurer of some kind. The first-floorers, who couldn't read or use Suikanet devices, saw the automated turnstiles as the maintainers of order, the agents that carried out the will of God. The sight of a person who had enslaved them to his will had an explosive effect on them.

One woman panicked and rushed to the third-floor escalator to seek instructions, where the first person she happened to speak to was Shido. He invited the traveler to the third floor to hear him out. The man was very fishy-looking, thirty or forty years old, with bulging eyes and glasses that only accentuated that further.

"It's nice to meet you. I am Keijin Nijo. I came from a city far to the north of here called Kyoto. I'm researching a method of shipping that uses the automated turnstiles, and this is my test run. Are you the representative of this village?" he asked, nearly shouting. His voice rang down the hallway. The people from the lower floors looked at Shido with fright in their eyes.

"No, but our representative hardly ever makes an appearance. I'm just a bioelectric technician," Shido explained, a little unsure of himself.

"I've never seen anyone force the turnstiles to move on their orders before. What kind of tech is that?"

As a third-floorer, Shido understood that the automated turnstiles were machines, not deities or devils, but it had never occurred to him that humans could control them. He supposed he was just ignorant, being from a rural settlement, and maybe this was normal in the cities.

"Well, I don't have total control of them. In short, I'm running a kind of Suikanet interference," the suspicious man detailed. "There are many automated turnstiles in Yokohama Station, and they move around Inside following certain algorithms. Let's say that two turnstiles come approaching each other, like *zwoop*. Ordinarily, when they recognize that they are approaching each other, both will turn on their heels and go the opposite direction. So if you give them something to carry, they will not ordinarily take it very far."

To demonstrate, the man held up fingers and moved them closer and farther apart.

"However, this is not because the turnstiles have designated areas they cover. My hypothesis is that the automated turnstiles do not possess the concept of individuality. In other words, they are all merely pieces of a single system. So when these two go *zwoop*, if I hit them—*bam!*—with a net interference signal, they go *swish*, and then *bada-boom*. Using this, I can give the turnstiles of Kyoto cargo to carry and get them to walk all this way with me. Of course, there's still some level of randomness to their actions, so I'll need a few other types of signals."

Keijin gesticulated wildly as he spoke. Shido had no idea what he meant, but he assumed that people talked like this in the big city. The strange man went on, regardless. He was accompanying the turnstiles on this test, but he would be able to send them alone to remote locations for trade and transport in the future. If he could make it possible to ship objects all over, not just send information on Suikanet, it might turn all of Yokohama Station into one coherent economic zone. And on, and on.

"There are tons and tons of automated turnstiles in Yokohama Station. They outnumber human beings. We can't give up the chance to incorporate them into our economy! That's what I think, at least."

With every few enthusiastic words, Keijin sprayed spittle, which was not very pleasant. Still, he was also enjoying himself and life in a way that Shido had never seen before. In the village, everyone seemed to think they existed only to fulfill the role that belonged to everyone on their floor. Even the family on the fifth level, who ruled over the settlement, was no different. Shido himself was merely another part of the system, a single organ in the being that was the village.

Shido informed someone on the fourth level about the strange man and told them that he sought an audience with the fifth-floor family. After a while, the answer came back—they would not meet with the bizarre fellow. A few days later, the turnstile whisperer was instructed to leave the village at once. The ruling family was afraid of revolution, and they wanted to avoid any upset of the established hierarchy, which held that the automated turnstiles were the very symbol of order.

"Well, I guess that's that. On to the next town," said Nijo to Shido. "By the way, I'm going to need help to continue developing my shipping business! People like you who are young, strong, and curious would be ideal. If you're interested, contact me here," he stated quickly. Then he gave Shido a business card with a Suikanet address on it.

The little thing had the man's name written in kanji, along with the strange phrase *Keijin 2Jo*. Shido could understand the kanji but had no idea what the other stuff meant.

This brief encounter would go on to change Shido's life dramatically.

4

The reason for Shido Kumano's exile from the village was quite simple. The son of the family that lived on the fifth floor had his eye on Shido's fiancée. He already had a wife from the fourth floor, but he also kept a few lovers on the third and second levels. Shido was a nuisance to him, and he cooked up an order of expulsion based on some violation that Shido had never committed. He recalled it containing difficult words like *rectitude*, *apostasy*, and *tempestuousness*. He definitely remembered that the decree had spelled his name *Shido Kumada*, which was wrong. There was no court or justice system in the settlement, of course. When someone from the fifth floor mandated something, there was no means to overturn it.

"You were such a good child. Why would God mistreat you so horribly?" Shido's mother wept. When she said "God," she was not talking about the fifth-floorer but actual, literal God. To the third-floorers, the decrees of the fifth-floor family, whom they virtually never met, were less like human decisions and closer to natural phenomena. It was the same for Shido—except that in his case, it was closer to the arrival of an entirely new, previously unknown season of the year.

Ever since meeting and speaking with the man who controlled the automated turnstiles, a desire had been building larger and larger in his subconscious—a wish to leave the village. And his exile was simply the first step to actually realizing it. Thus, he gathered his belongings and decided to go several days earlier than the deadline indicated on the edict. The only note he left behind was for Mimi.

You did nothing wrong.

He had absolutely nowhere else to go, so his first goal was to find the man named Keijin Nijo. Shido had no idea if the man's offer to hire him was still good, as it had been years. But he tried to contact the address on the business card anyway. The only response he received was a message that the address was no longer in use. Suikanet addresses could change on their own, simply from the station's expansion. There was nothing more to be done about it, so Shido elected to make for Kyoto instead. Whether Keijin was there or not, he presumed he'd find work in the city.

There was no reason to rush the journey, so Shido avoided the escalator slopes on the mountains, first heading downhill and then slowly north through the Nara Basin, performing contract work where he went, and seeing various ruins and other famous sites.

"There are many ancient tombstones around these parts," said an old man he met in Asuka, pointing at the wall. The facades in that area were completely unlike the standard concrete walls of Yokohama Station. Yet they were much stranger than the natural stone you could see in movies. The best way Shido could describe it was natural rock that had been cut into rectangular shapes.

"Long, long, long ago, this place used to be the tomb of royalty. This stone comes from that era," the old man explained.

According to the vague knowledge Shido had picked up reading historical novels, the ancient kings ruled over this area over two thousand years ago, long before Yokohama Station took over. He didn't know why this stone would be inside the station, but he listened to the elderly man's story with great interest.

Because he took many detours, Shido didn't reach Kyoto until about a month after his exile.

Like other basins Inside, Kyoto became a stratified city as Yokohama Station filled the empty space between the high ground. What set it apart from places like Kofu, however, was that its corridors were extremely orderly, generated in a neat lattice pattern. The structural genetic field incorporated the memory of the original grid-based city and built layer upon layer in that pattern.

According to his last correspondence, Keijin's place of business was Kitaoji, Horikawa, Kanoetora 7. Physical addresses in Kyoto had three coordinates, indicating north-south, east-west, and up-down. Kitaoji was near the city's northern edge, Horikawa was slightly east of the center, and Kanoetora referred to the 27th level. Presently, the highest floor in Kyoto was Kinoeuma (the 31st), so Kanoetora was very high up. He'd heard that the strata in Kyoto were not a literal hierarchy the way they were in his village, but Shido understood that the wealthy still tended to live higher up. Keijin's business was doing well.

In most cities, the haphazard development of Yokohama Station made addresses a source of confusion above all else, so Kyoto's orderly, systematic address style was a true wonder in motion. Shido's village was small enough that they possessed no concept of an address.

But when he reached the spot the address indicated, Keijin was not there. The lot belonged to a tofu restaurant. The restaurant manager said that the previous owner had sold the place three years ago, and he didn't know where they'd gone. Shido tried asking around in the area, but it sounded as though the turnstile-based shipping business went up in smoke, and no one knew where Keijin was.

That left Shido to find a different source of work. Unfortunately, Kyoto was cold to outsiders, and he did not have anyone to vouch for him, so it was difficult to find honest employment. His area of expertise was Suika installation, but that was a job where trust was paramount, and no one would ask a wanderer like Shido to do such a sensitive process.

He settled in the lower-level slums, looking for contract jobs to get by, eventually becoming a delivery man for a tobacco seller. His role was to take the cigarettes discovered in vending machines here and there to station hollows in places like Arashiyama and Mt. Hiei. Smoking was forbidden Inside, so the station hollows closest to the big cities became de facto smoking areas. The work came with a lot of hassles if the police caught you, so highly expendable people like Shido were perfectly suited to it.

There were two police forces in Kyoto while Shido was there. The east and west sides of the city were managed by different groups, known as the left and right police. Each side justified its style while vilifying the other as illegitimate.

The left police claimed that they traced their lineage directly from the Kyoto Police that existed in the Japanese government era. The right police, meanwhile, insisted that the Kyoto Police perished in the Winter War, and thus their rival's assertion was totally fabricated. Instead, *they* were the offshoot of the vigilante force that came together to maintain order in the post-war chaos. The actual civilians under their protection didn't care, of course, and only wanted the two sides to knock it off.

There were subtle legal differences between the opposing factions. The left police outlawed tobacco and collected fines from those in possession, while the right considered it legal but subject to heavy taxation. A cigarette courier was responsible for all monetary losses.

"The worst is if they catch you on Suzaku Avenue," an older courier told Shido. Both left and right police wandered around that centralized area, so if one side got you, the other was soon to follow, and you'd have to pay them both.

One day, in the first month of Shido's job, he got caught by a left police officer named Higashiyama, who found the cigarettes under his clothes. Shido resigned himself to paying the fee of 30,000 milliyen, but the low-ranking officer stopped him and said, "Make an individual payment to my Suika for ten thousand milliyen, and I'll let you go." Naturally, Shido agreed to that.

Higashiyama had been employed by the left police for many years, but his arrogant attitude kept him from getting any promotions. For extra income, he took bribes from organized criminals. Shido made regular payments to him and received information about left police patrol routes in return. All they did was robotically follow designated routes the Suikanet gave them, so as long as he knew the paths ahead of time, he didn't have to worry about them. After that, Shido enjoyed success as a transporter, and his boss had reason to remember his name.

He continued carrying cigarettes until he knew quite a bit about the Kyoto underworld, and eventually, he heard a few rumors about Keijin Nijo. A turnstile-based shipping business would make it safer to transport cigarettes and more dangerous drugs, so the fate of his operation was of great interest. However, the man had shuttered his place three years earlier, and no one knew where he was. Fortunately, he had a daughter named Keiha, who wasn't even twenty yet, and she still lived in Kyoto.

Shido paid Higashiyama some money to access the citizen database using his police privileges, which was how he learned that Keiha Nijo lived at Rokujo Karasuma Kanoeuma, on the seventh floor of the city.

5

"The poor girl. Her mother went of illness when she was eight, and her father followed after when she was fifteen," Modori Tanaka told Shido.

Keijin Nijo's daughter, Keiha, lived on Kanoeuma, the seventh floor of Kyoto, with an older woman named Modori. She was an old friend of Keiha's mother, and she had taken in Keiha after the girl lost her parents.

Their residence was a spacious one-floor unit, one commonly seen in Inside cities. Keiha's personal space was segmented off with a screen that was not particularly tall, so Shido could see what she was up to even when sitting at the table.

"Kei? This man is a friend of your father's," said Modori. Keiha glanced over at Shido, silently bowed her head, then turned back to the large display on her desk and began to type fervently on the keyboard.

She wore thick glasses and a tracksuit, and her long hair hung all the way to the back of her chair. She was eighteen years old, but unlike the other city girls her age, she kept the vibrancy of her youth locked away.

"Do you mind if I ask you about what happened to Keijin?" Shido inquired. Modori glanced at Keiha, then described the events in a low voice.

Keijin's transport system using automated turnstiles caught the attention of Kyoto's criminal elements. The police couldn't do anything about turnstiles, which made it the perfect method for moving tobacco and harder drugs. Keijin did not have significant qualms about this particular use of his system, either, apparently. He was an engineer's engineer, through and through.

However, between the desires of several criminal cliques and the two police groups, the dealings and motives got very tangled indeed, and the man at the center of all the wrangling wound up shot with an electric pump gun. The shooter was a young trooper from a drug-smuggling ring that was a rival to the one Shido worked for. The automated turnstiles promptly dumped him into Lake Biwa.

Shido had read about murders in old mystery novels before, but he couldn't hide his shock at hearing the story of a real one. When someone killed another person Inside, the turnstiles would come and clean it up right away, so the concept of the "murder case" found in novels didn't exist here.

"If only he'd kept his nose out of those inventions and stayed home to watch after Kei," Modori said wistfully.

Despite a moment of hesitation, Shido explained, "I was born in a village on the south end of the Kii Peninsula. That's where I met Keijin."

He recounted his background and the system of the place where he grew up.

"When I was younger, I never understood what a horrible village it was. The lower-floorers were always at the bottom. Even on the middle floors, everything was decided for us before we were born. But I didn't know anything about the outside world, so I just assumed that was normal. Learning about the existence of someone like Keijin, who started his own business with only his tech knowledge and freely traveled around Inside—it saved my life, honestly. I'd hazard to say that people in other places experienced the same feeling I did just by coming into contact with him."

These words were his true feelings, and he hoped they might serve as some small measure of comfort to a girl whose father was cruelly ripped away from her.

However, Shido did not mention his current alignment with the Kyoto underworld. Modori mumbled and made little statements to fill the silence, like "Oh, that must have been hard."

The state of food production and other living infrastructure was good all over Kyoto. Even those in the lower classes were rarely ever in want of the basic elements of survival. Still, Kanoeuma and the floors below it had the atmosphere of slums. You often saw people resting in a lifeless daze on flattened cardboard boxes in the hallways. Some had spouses and made children, but they knew from the start that they could never afford the 500,000 milliyen the kid would need. They had no hope to look forward to. The few scraps of money they earned went into the cigarettes that Shido's gang dealt or were frittered away on lottery tickets run by other criminal groups.

There was no real violent disorder in the city, so it wasn't just the poor who lived on this level, but also frugal types, which was the category Modori Tanaka seemed to fall into. Shido knew from experience that people like her did not think highly of the underworld society.

Modori offered to serve dinner and went out to buy food, leaving Shido and Keiha behind. Shido kept glancing awkwardly at Keiha, trying and failing to think of something to break the silence. She paid him almost no mind, typing away at the keyboard and plugging and unplugging cables from strange machines. Shido stared at the TV screen on the wall, wishing Modori would return soon.

Suikanet broadcasts of late were full of news about JR North Japan. Stories about the people of Hokkaido outside of Yokohama Station's grasp were stirring up tensions in the northernmost part of the station. Supposedly, outsiders were crossing the Tsugaru Strait to kidnap Inside children. Inside maintained a fundamental noninterest in the JRs, but when it came to harming the residents, there was understandably some anger. Of course, that rage was impotent, as no one had any means of doing anything to JR North Japan across the strait.

"According to our station's exclusive sources, even the media in Hokkaido is outraged by these actions," the news claimed. Reports on Suikanet were not organized and sent out by some core agency. Instead, they were mechanically collected from all over and transmitted according to frequency. It took three days for information from the Tsugaru Strait to reach Kyoto, and Shido had no way of knowing what "our station" was or if it was a trustworthy source.

Idly, he considered the outside world. Yokohama Station was already expanding in Shikoku, but Hokkaido and Kyushu were purportedly maintaining their defense lines. He wondered why they would need to protect their lands to the point of kidnapping Insiders. Wasn't it much more pleasant Inside, rather than being exposed to all the rain and wind of the outdoors?

"About your village," Keiha began out of the blue. It took Shido several seconds to recognize that it was her voice and not part of the news program. It was calm and low in pitch. "You said the rulers of the village got their money from somewhere and paid it to the lower classes for their labor?"

"...Y-yes," Shido replied.

"I think they must have a milliyen miner."

"Miner?"

"When the population of Yokohama Station increases, the Suika implementation means paying another five hundred thousand milliyen to the net, right? If that process repeats enough times, it will eventually exhaust the supply of milliyen. Haven't you ever thought that was strange?"

"That's a good point. I've never considered it before in my life, but it *is* strange."

"Well, that's because there are machines that mine the milliyen that are lost, thus returning them to the money supply. They were all made a long, long time ago, but I'd assume the one in your village is still functional."

"What do you mean, mining? Are there buried milliyen somewhere in the form of coins, like the money in the old times?" Shido asked, recalling his own job of scavenging cigarettes for money.

"No. For one thing, milliyen don't have a physical form. Suika milliyen are simply a history of transactions that are sent through Suika-net, indicating which Suika has how much of a balance, and so on. There are several complex encryption systems working in the background, and not particularly complicated calculations guarantee the encryption. So to make more milliyen, you need a special kind of device. I call that a miner, although I've never seen one before. That's how those people were able to offer money endlessly, and thus order around everyone else."

Shido didn't quite understand what Keiha was talking about. He was more startled by the way that, after holding her silence for so long, she'd suddenly burst into a fountain of words. Her manner of speaking with no regard to the listener's comprehension struck him as similar to her father, Keijin.

"You know about some very complicated subjects," he remarked.

It did not cause much of a change in her demeanor. "Anyway, here's my real question: Do you hate those people who ruled over you and kicked you out?"

"Actually, to tell the truth, I wasn't that sad about it. Once I met Keijin, I was more interested in seeing the city. I think it was a greater disaster for my parents and Mimi."

"So you feel that it was a 'disaster,' specifically?"

"Er, no. It was the work of human beings, of course. It's just that society is always plagued by some kind of unfairness that can strike like a natural event. It's something we just have to live under, I suppose," answered Shido.

Keiha made an extremely displeased face, then rotated the large monitor on her desk to face him. "Here, this is a system I created."

In the center of the black screen was a white circle with lines extending outward.

"With a bit of concentrated interference from Suikanet nodes in the vicinity of a miner, you can render them incapable of mining milliyen. Or, to be more accurate, it puts an extreme load on the node the miner is connected to, which scatters the mined milliyen all around. I made the thing but couldn't test it because I didn't know where to find any miners. If you want revenge on the people ruling your village, I'd like to mess with their miner. Could you tell me where to find it?"

"W-wait, just a moment." Shido held up his hands to stop her. "Don't just rush through with this. First of all, this miner thing? You don't even know if there is one in the village. I've never heard of any such thing."

"Then we'll try running the device to find out if they've got one or not. Nothing will happen if they don't."

"Listen, that's not the problem… And for one thing, what reason would you have for doing this?"

"I want to find out if my system works or not. I'll need it eventually."

"What do you mean?"

"I'll explain later. I'm just saying that I have this tool. Do you want me to use it?"

Shido considered this. "First of all, the village has its own circumstances. I don't feel right about manipulating its fate for my own personal reasons."

"But think about it. The people who rule your village control everyone else just because they happen to own a miner. It seems only fair that someone with an interference device exploits *them* for a bit, don't you think?"

"You're being stupid. That's not a valid reason," Shido snapped. It seemed to intimidate Keiha, for she fell silent. "Listen, this might be cruel to say to a girl I just met today, but I think you've been through a lot in life despite still being young, and it's made you a little bit crazy. I can tell that Modori's right, and you're very smart, but once you get older, I think you'll see more of the logic of how society—"

"Enough about me," she interrupted. "It's simple. Your family and your former fiancée underwent a 'disaster.' You might have the means to help them now. So you should probably try. Wouldn't you agree?"

That kind of made sense to him. However, Shido got the feeling this girl was seeing him as nothing more than a machine that would act on her orders, and when he saw her looking at him, that was exactly what he glimpsed in her eyes.

About two months after that, he received a Suikanet message from his family back in the village. The exile edict had previously forbidden them from contacting Shido, so the presence of any message suggested the mandate had been repealed.

According to his parents, the fifth-floor residents had vanished from the village all of a sudden. Rumors were they had been lax on their milliyen payments, leading to widespread distrust from the rest of the settlement. After some discussion, the fourth-floor families decided upon a new system of government, and the edict to have Shido exiled was no more. They wanted him to come back home and said that Mimi wished to see him, too. Shido considered his response carefully.

"I'm in Kyoto now. I'm leading a comfortable life and have many friends. I'm very happy to hear that I'm welcome in the village again. I have some things to do here, so I won't be back for a while. I'm sorry. Say hello to Mimi for me."

Shido reported what had happened back home to Keiha, who did something she'd never done before—looked happy.

"Okay. So the milliyen redistribution function works. Next up, the automated turnstiles."

She began to type on her keyboard. Shido considered that maybe she wasn't just a poor unfortunate girl who lost her parents too young, but that she was something else entirely, strange and unfathomable. And he was caught in her snare.

"What are you planning to do?" Shido asked.

"Nothing that serious," the young woman replied.

6

"The first step will be uniting the left and right police. It doesn't need to be a public alliance, though, so we'll just bring one representative member of each along. Got any individuals in mind?" Keiha said, staring at the screen. On the monitor was a list of the principal organizations in Kyoto, both legitimate and underground. Shido's tobacco smuggling ring was among the entries.

"In the left police, I know a guy named Higashiyama. He's a real dirty scumbag of a cop. I pay him, and he gives me police intel."

"Sounds useful. Can we get him on board?"

"He won't say no if we can guarantee him a good rank. That's the kind of person he is. I'm not so familiar with the right police, but I can ask our member who handles the west side for advice."

"Please do. I can't negotiate with them, so having you around will really help out."

"Sure," he agreed, scratching at his beard bashfully. He'd been growing out his facial hair, hoping a gruffer look would help him at his job, but it was itchy, and Keiha had stated, "You look like a wild bear now."

Two years had passed since control in Shido's hometown had changed hands. The class system of the village had all but vanished. Mimi married a man who'd been on the second floor originally, and his sixty-something father passed away of old age. His mother insisted that he come home for the funeral, but Shido used his busy schedule as an excuse not to return.

Truthfully, he was ashamed to show himself. But even more than that, he really was that busy. In the past two years, Shido had risen in the ranks and now ran the cigarette smuggling operation. That wasn't because of his contribution, actually, but the result of Keiha's net interference. In an organization that had evolved to be highly systematic and complex, control over online information made it relatively easy to earn a particular individual greater status.

"When work calms down, I'll come see you," Shido assured his mother, but he couldn't imagine when such a time might arrive. Things were only becoming more demanding. Keiha had control over most of the Suikanet nodes in the Kyoto area, and she was currently able to manipulate the actions of the automated turnstiles to a limited extent.

"So what exactly do you do to control the net? Understanding that I'm probably too stupid to get it," Shido asked Keiha one day.

"Well…" She leaned hard against the backrest of her chair until her long hair threatened to touch the floor. "First of all, do you know how Suikanet moves information around?"

"Nope."

"Well, of course you don't. Even I don't really get it," she replied, without a trace of shame. Shido's eyes bulged. "Nobody comprehends the precise details. It's something that Yokohama Station generated on its own, so there are no protocols written down anywhere. All I know for sure is that the structural genetic field absorbed the mechanisms that the original internet and JR Integrated Intelligence used, and it replicated them."

According to her explanation, Yokohama Station was full of countless things called Suikanet nodes. They connected and interacted with one another in a netlike formation, which was why it was called Suikanet. Nobody knew what physical form these nodes took, because they were embedded deep into the physical structure of the station. Only by indirect online access could anyone confirm their existence.

The information you could glean by accessing the net was typically whatever data was accumulated in the nearest node. Nodes synchronized their contents through communication, but the reliability of that correspondence was so poor that most data updating was done by majority rule. In other words, if a node written with A was connected to ten nodes, eight of which said B, that node would be overwritten to state B.

By interfering with this intranodal communication, if you overwrote all the information going into a specific node with C, you could create a C node, when such a thing did not previously exist on Suikanet. Doing so to multiple nodes forced C to spread outward through the system.

However, protocols were largely unknown, and they also differed slightly by region, so putting this into practice was far from easy. Still, Keiha had been doing it for so long (with the benefit of inheriting her father's work) that she was now able to overwrite nearly all the nodes in Kyoto as she pleased.

And Shido knew from personal experience that if she could successfully control Suikanet, Keiha could easily manipulate the human society that depended on it to operate. After all, she'd brought an end to the dictatorship that ruled his hometown by commanding the flow of milliyen. Without the station's control, the Insiders were so incredibly powerless.

More and more people came and went from Keiha's home on the Kanoeuma level. Several representatives from the left and right police assembled to discuss the shape of the combined police force, the results of which were then sent all over Kyoto through the net. The underworld groups did largely the same thing. Keiha reserved ultimate veto rights over whatever was decided, but she hardly ever offered any input on the means of city management.

Her mother figure, Modori, saw the many visitors to her withdrawn daughter and delighted over the attention. "I'm so glad she's made some friends." She seemed to have almost no idea what Keiha was actually doing. She'd seemingly aged quite a lot in the last few years, so telling her that the girl was pretty much running all of Kyoto would probably be a bit too much of a shock for the woman.

Unlike her father, Keiha had almost no interest in forming relationships with trustworthy people. Therefore, Shido, who had good social skills and close connections with both sides of the law, became Keiha's most trusted confidant in running the suspicious group.

Shido was aware that he was being used by a girl over a decade his junior and of how she'd grown from a child into a woman as the little society matured. To the people who gathered at her house—especially the later ones to join—Keiha was almost a holy presence, like a shrine maiden from the ancient days of religious rule. Her influence was expanding beyond Kyoto into the neighboring regions.

"I'd like a name," she stated one day.

"A name?"

"Yes. A name for our group. Higashiyama and some of the others are insisting on it. I'm not so good at that sort of thing. You come up with it."

Shido considered this for just a few seconds before saying, "Why not call it the Dodger Alliance?"

"Dodger?"

"I was just thinking of a product that our group handles," Shido explained, pulling out a slender pipe with a bit of metal on either end and a long wooden stem in the middle. "It's a tool for smoking tobacco. When I was younger, the books I read named an ancient practice of cheating your station fare after these pipes. Tricksters would buy tickets for the start and end of their trip, but not for any of the transfers in between. I guess people thought it was like how the pipe only has metal on the ends. I just happened to have one of them on hand, and it reminded me of that old practice, that's all."

"That's a beautiful design. Very well, Dodger Alliance it is."

The people of the city never knew about the existence of the Dodger Alliance. To outward appearances, the left and right police continued to bicker over territory. In truth, though, both sides were under Keiha's control, so any trouble that arose was settled with internal discussions. Police taxes were no longer levied twice. That alone made a noticeable improvement in the lives of the citizens. Economic indicators rose, and work was ample, even for the poorer people on the lower levels. The entire city was full of life.

Shido could feel that their control was beneficial for all. The people who'd ruled over his village had social power simply because they'd possessed a mining device, and they'd only used it to satisfy their selfish desires.

Yet Keiha could hardly be less interested in her strength over the city government as the ruling member of their secretive council. She was only enthusiastic about acquiring control over Suikanet nodes with her tools and tech. In time, Shido sensed that her lust for expansion without definition shared something in common with Yokohama Station itself.

Because of that, Shido learned a valuable lesson when the Dodger Alliance met its sudden conclusion: When the end arrives, it comes quickly and without warning.

Keiha brought about the abrupt upheaval of the ruling structure in Shido's village, and her own organization fell apart just as swiftly. Therefore, he reasoned that the unruly growth of the station itself would one day meet its end quickly, too.

And it would happen as easily and simply as a single grain of sand dropping to the ground.

7

"Osaka?"

"Yes. We've pretty much finished acquiring all the net nodes around there, so the station employees in the area wanted us to send over a representative of the alliance. Could you leave tomorrow?" Keiha asked, holding the electric kettle.

"This is quite sudden," Shido replied. It took an entire day to walk from Kyoto to Osaka.

"It'll take a while, I'm thinking. Many kinds of people live there.

Controlling the net will be a lot easier than all of them. I'll need someone trustworthy to go."

"Got it."

Osaka was once the second-largest metropolis in Japan, but with Honshu covered by Yokohama Station, it had lost its past glory. The structural genetic field found it easier to build up stratified cities in basins. However, because Osaka possessed such a highly developed rail network and the stations were so much denser than in other regions, the concentration of Suikanet nodes was tremendously high. Seizing them all was a pain, but they would be tough to wrest from the hand that held them later, making the region a valuable base.

The screen on Keiha's desk displayed the nodes they presently controlled.

"How far are you going to expand?" Shido questioned. Keiha's nodes were shown in green on the digital map of Japan. The range of nodes was expanding by the day and currently spanned from Osaka Bay to the east shore of Lake Biwa. He didn't know what it actually meant to acquire control over Suikanet; Shido was purely impressed with the level of Keiha's ability to achieve so much.

She did not answer his inquiry, however. She just poured green tea from the pot into two cups.

"Want some?" she asked, handing him one.

"Thank you," Shido replied, carefully taking the cup. Keiha had dutifully waited for the boiled water to fall to one hundred and sixty degrees before steeping the tea, so the cup wasn't all that hot to the touch.

"Well, I guess it doesn't matter. Anyway," Shido said, pointing at the right side of the map. "There are some big gaps. Why did you seize these spots out in the mountains?"

Farther away from the Kansai cities, there were some volcanoes like Mt. Haku, Mt. Ontake, and Mt. Asama, where Keiha had captured several nodes. Compared to their control over their own territory, the dots were tiny and isolated.

"That wasn't me. Dad did that."

"Keijin did?"

"Yes. When he was young, he said he could use Suikanet to predict disasters, and he scooped up the nodes around the mountains. These are leftovers from that."

"Like...eruptions?"

Keiha took a sip of the tea. "The nodes Dad claimed were on a much smaller scale than mine, but they're all extremely tough. I haven't touched them in over a decade, but they're still firmly uncontested. My nodes, on the other hand, can't be left alone for more than a few months, or else neighboring nodes will reclaim them."

"Uh-huh..."

Silence settled between the pair for a minute. Shido watched the specks of tea move about the inside of the cup, thinking what he should say.

"This might be a strange thing to ask, but...what was it like having him for a father?"

"I don't know."

"Huh?"

"He was always out traveling. Hardly spent any time in Kyoto. Every now and then, he'd send a huge amount of data back home."

"Data?"

"Yes. He would report back with his new discoveries about the structure of Suikanet and its Codama language. It was just after Mom died, so that would have been when I was eight."

"He sent that back to his eight-year-old daughter?" Shido exclaimed, distressed.

"Is that odd?" Keiha asked. By the light of the glossy screen, he could see that her expression was perfectly serious.

"Even knowing how smart you are, it's strange."

"But isn't it normal for parents to teach their children about things necessary for survival?"

There was no doubt that Keiha's abilities were potent within the environment of the Inside world, but that didn't seem to connect to "survival." Shido had to think before he answered.

"Hmm. That's a good point. My family was a line of bioelectric technicians. When I finished school, they taught me how to do Suika implants. In my village, you couldn't choose your profession, so that was a skill I needed to survive."

He assumed that was how she meant it. However, her father had been murdered because his tech had proved a little too effective.

Keiha continued to zoom in and out on the map of Japan. It was like she was reassuring herself of what her father had left behind for her.

"Is that hole a volcano?" Shido inquired, pointing at the screen. Around the center of Mt. Ontake, there was a black region with absolutely no Suikanet nodes. Based on the legend, the hole was about a kilometer across. For an inland station hollow, that was huge.

"No. That's an exit. See where it says Exit 42?"

"Exit 42?"

"Strange, right? Yokohama Station's exits are numbered in the order they're generated, so the smaller numbers should all be in the Kanagawa area, where the city is. Why would it be out in Nagano? My father had nothing written about that in his notes."

"It probably wasn't important enough to mark down. Weird things like that happen Inside all the time, don't they? For example, the hallway where it says 'Nara Line Ruins' is in Kyoto, not Nara," said Shido, chuckling.

Keiha suddenly turned very grave. "Shido, the fact that exit numbers are consistent across all of Yokohama Station suggests there is a functioning core that maintains the entire station. If each regional structure in different areas handed out exit numbers, there would be redundant numbers all over the place."

"Core?"

"Something like the brain or heart, in human terms. In other words, the big question is, is the station structured like a plant, as a collection of localized modules? Or is it structured like an animal, split between core functions and terminal points? Perhaps this strange exit is a hint to the answer."

"Uh-huh," Shido replied. "So ultimately, you're hoping to go and seize that core. And then you'll be able to take control over all of Yokohama Station."

"Do you think so?" Keiha asked. She seemed a little sad for some reason.

That was the very last day Shido saw Keiha in person. Whenever he thought back on her, it was that slightly forlorn expression that came to mind.

8

The moment of truth arrived when Shido left for Osaka on Keiha's orders, finished his job there, and was on his way back. He received an emergency communication from Keiha.

She'd told him that it was possible to engage in voice communication long-distance using Suikanet, but this was the first time he'd ever seen it work. It was an ominous sign.

"Don't come back to Kyoto. It's bad. Get as far away as you can," she instructed. Her tone of voice was just as relaxed as it always was, but he could make out the sound of rapid breathing in the background.

"What do you mean? Get away from what?"

"From Yokohama Station."

"…That's impossible. What happened?"

"I'm losing control over the automated turnstiles. The reactions from all of our Suikas are going wrong. We've probably been declared illegitimate. They took Mom away."

"Modori? She had almost nothing to do with the alliance's activities."

"Just flee from the station, as far as you can. I'm going to find some kind of countermeasure. Stay alive until then."

Then Keiha ended the communication. That was the last time Shido and Keiha ever spoke.

Not long after, Shido's Suika stopped receiving net access. The automated turnstiles showed up and nabbed him, and they tossed him onto the coast of Osaka Bay.

Awaji Island wasn't totally Stationized yet, and there were pirates without Suikas who made their base on the islands in Osaka Bay. They captured Shido and sold him to Shikoku as a source of labor. He was transported over the exposed ground in a terribly shaky vehicle called an automobile until he was assigned to do earthworks at a port in Takamatsu.

He understood from reference materials that human beings built structures in the outside world, and it sounded exotic and exciting enough. Performing the process in person was an excruciating experience, though. The civil engineering foreman struck him with a baton all the time. It was his first time being beaten, and he found the mental anguish to be even worse than the physical pain.

After that, Shido waited for his chance to steal a little boat and escape to sea, which was when he came to the island with the station spore upon it. Shikoku knew about the island, but because of the eerie appearance of the spore, they feared it and considered it even more frightening than Inside. Shido found the abandoned container house there and settled in it.

And he'd remained there ever since. He had no way of knowing what had happened to Keiha and the other alliance members.

◆

"...Why were you kicked out?" Haikunterke asked. Shido's story had ended rather abruptly.

He looked down in a daze and answered, "I don't know. It was very sudden at the end. Felt like waking up from a long dream. I'd lived in that little village in the country for so long that I wasn't sure which part had been the dream at first. Did the Dodger Alliance really exist? Did Keiha? Had I hallucinated the entire experience when I was exiled from the village? I was on the run from the automated turnstiles, and once I saw the Seto Inland Sea, I was finally able to accept that all of it was real."

"You mean when all of your Suikas were rendered illegitimate."

"From what I know, at the very least, turnstiles will exile individuals who have committed crimes, but they've never rolled up an entire group to kick them out as one," Shido said.

Such an event did not appear in JR North Japan's accumulated knowledge of Inside, either. For one thing, an "organization" was such an intangible concept that for Yokohama Station to selectively exile all of its members meant it possessed some means of understanding and tracking the interpersonal relationships of its residents. And that was a very frightening hypothesis to consider.

But there was no point in telling this man that.

"What was she trying to do anyway?" wondered Haikunterke. The rain was still falling heavily outside, filling the container's interior with uneasy noise, as there was almost nothing to absorb it.

"That was a mystery to me, too. I was with Keiha from the start to the collapse of the alliance, and she never once spoke about what her goals were. The other members talked of liberation from Yokohama Station's rule, but she wasn't the type of person to dream about things like that."

All of his experiences with her had taught him that. Keiha's ability with technology surpassed even her father's, but she didn't seem to share his interest in expansive, long-term plans, like transforming all of Yokohama Station's economy. All she did was collect the things she saw and judged to be necessary to her. Shido was more or less the number two man in the alliance, and it seemed like he was only in that position because he happened to be the first person to visit her home.

"After being exiled from Yokohama Station, I started to figure it out, though. I think she just wanted to protect herself. The machinations of a number of different groups within the city intersected in a way that got her father killed. She realized that the system governed by automated turnstiles wouldn't protect her or her family. So to her, taking over the entire city was the very minimum amount of self-defense she needed to feel secure."

"And the result was that she made an enemy out of Yokohama Station itself."

"Yes. So I feel certain that Keiha's out there somewhere, plotting how to defeat Yokohama Station. That's what she feels she needs to do now," Shido stated, quite seriously. Haikunterke almost burst into laughter. Fortunately, she was incapable of producing such an advanced emotional demonstration; she merely scrunched up her cheeks and nose in an odd way.

"That's impossible, even with extremely powerful methods of Suika-net interference. You can't destroy hardware by being knowledgeable about the software."

Especially not as an individual. Up north, they'd spent years and years fighting just to keep Yokohama Station isolated to the Seikan Tunnel.

"You aren't really from Shikoku, are you?" Shido asked Haikunterke. "You know a lot about the net and automated turnstiles. There's no way someone from there would understand so much, especially a child. Were you born Inside, too?"

"...No."

"Would you be willing to tell me who you really are?"

"I'm sorry. I can't do that."

"All right. Sorry if I was being insensitive."

They fell silent. For a long time, there was only the rain.

"Just let me ask one thing," she said.

"Yes?"

"At the end of your story, Keiha was investigating that strange exit near the volcano, wasn't she?"

"That's right. She called it Exit 42."

Haikunterke had a feeling that was the case. In the process of learning more about the exit, she came into contact with something that wasn't meant to be found, and that's why she was exiled from Inside, along with anyone connected to her.

But it was a truth too cruel to tell this man. He still believed the woman's guarantee that she would find a solution.

Several nights later, Haikunterke returned to the house with her data collection on the station spore more or less complete and found Shido burning up with fever. He'd been in poor health to begin with, but even he admitted that this was worse than he'd ever experienced before.

"I've been kicked out of all sorts of places. Guess the only place left to get kicked out of is life itself," he said bitterly.

"Don't speak. Here's some water."

Haikunterke was worried. Her supplemental memory device contained a passing amount of medical knowledge. Still, the android hadn't expected she'd need to make use of it at all Inside and had seldom reflected upon it. She'd have to read and affix it to her main memory from scratch. It would be like operating an unfamiliar machine with only a hefty manual for reference.

What would Samayunkur do? she wondered, as she had often done Inside. She didn't have the luxury to stop and consider it this time. Haikunterke consulted Shido's symptoms.

"I think it's a cellular disease—the kind with insects or birds as a vector. There's only one human being on this island, after all," she said briefly. Shido's wits were hazy, but it seemed as though the look in his eyes was one of understanding. "There are multiple potential affliction names, but the particular cures for all of them are unlikely to be available on this island. They weren't among the matter that building produces, either."

Shido smiled, his face bright.

"I see. Uh-huh. That seems right." He paused for a moment. "Thank you, Terke. I enjoyed getting the chance to talk to someone again."

Then he drank a bit of water and slowly fell unconscious.

Haikunterke remained in contact with her supplemental memory device, doing everything she possibly could to counteract the symptoms of the general type of infection Shido had. After a while, the android began to wonder why she was doing so much to take care of this human. She'd only been playing the role of an escaped girl from Shikoku to investigate the spore without attracting suspicion.

Once she'd done all she could, Haikunterke sat a short distance away from the bed and whispered, "You probably can't hear me anymore, but I'll tell you about myself." Shido gave no reaction, and she continued, "I'm a saboteur sent from JR North Japan. I was built to resemble a human being, but my body is entirely mechanical.

"Our headquarters has been fighting for ages to protect our land from the expansion of Yokohama Station. Our technology has developed greatly over the years, and we can now create weapons that destroy the station structure and android agents capable of reaching the other side of the station. My companions are all over Inside, searching for a way to stop Yokohama Station from advancing. My mission brought me all this way.

"However, it doesn't seem like there *is* a way to end it. The structural genetic field continues to evolve, and the more our tech advances, the more resources we expend. We're going to run out of options soon. It's causing the relationship between engineering and the other divisions to worsen."

Haikunterke stopped to think for a second.

"I've never had the desire to preserve or protect myself. I was born with a purpose to fulfill. Survival is merely a means to achieve my mission. But living things aren't like that. Because existence itself is the goal, life has flourished on this planet for billions of years. Which do you suppose is better?"

"...Ahh."

Shido's mouth moved. Haikunterke stopped talking.

"Oh, Keiha. Where are you now? I want to see you..."

He seemed to be muttering incoherently.

When the sun rose the next day, Haikunterke carried the raft she'd beached on the hill down to the island's southern shore.

Her data collection of the station spore was complete, and she'd spent more than enough time for Suikanet's immune memory of her to fade. There was no reason to stay any longer. Next, she needed to land on Shikoku and cross the Great Seto Bridge to investigate and confirm the present expansion of the station. Most importantly of all, she could not simply sit around with nothing to do, because it was a waste of the special body she'd been granted.

"I don't think it'll work," she said, facing the direction of the container house where Shido slept. His fever had receded, and she'd left him some water and food, so he would be able to manage from there.

But my guesses are usually wrong. I hope you see her again, she thought.

As Haikunterke surrendered to the current of the Seto Inland Sea, she pondered what it meant when human beings prayed.

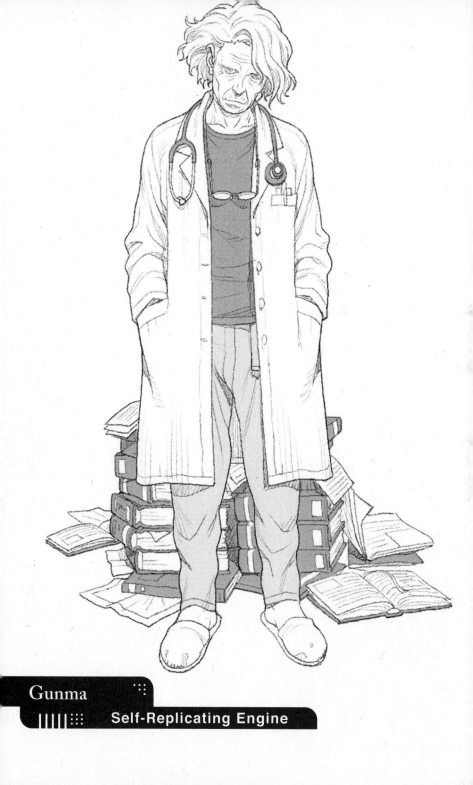

Gunma
||||| ::: Self-Replicating Engine

1

Station Year 178, Western Gunma

"Dr. Blue-Eyes, we've got trouble."

A bug-eyed young man came hurtling in from the adjacent room so suddenly that the white-haired man he called Dr. Blue-Eyes nearly dropped his coffee cup onto the floor.

Many of the rooms Yokohama Station generated were designed to be commercial storefronts and tended to be more open than spaces intended for domestic living. So Dr. Blue-Eyes's clinic-cum-dwelling had no door, just a few bookcases arranged near the hallway to give him a modicum of privacy.

"I've told you how many times, Nijo: When you're in a rush, knock first."

"But, Doctor, you don't have a door."

"Do it on this," Blue-Eyes insisted, rapping the back of the metal bookcase. The young man's face lit up with sudden enlightenment, and he nodded eagerly.

"Anyway, we've got trouble. And when I say trouble, I mean upheaval, as in great change. We are literally upheaving, sir."

"Right. First of all, calm down."

"This is normal for me, sir. Um, anyway, look at this. This right here."

The bug-eyed young man named Nijo placed a laptop device on Dr. Blue-Eyes's table and opened it. There was a map of the Gunma area on the screen; a triangular symbol indicating a mountain was in the center.

"For the last year, I've been measuring the communication range of the Suikanet nodes around this mountain to the south. And in the last few days, the physical distance between the nodes implanted in various regions of the station structure has been expanding. It's growing, like *zoooop*," the young man explained, pulling his hands apart. The action caused him to smack his hand against a bookcase due to the cramped interior, but he didn't seem to mind.

"What's your point?"

"The station structure around here is expanding. And I think it's growing in the lower levels, causing the upper levels to warp and shift," he said. Then he brought up an interior map of the station and pointed out the lower altitudes.

"That is not possible, Nijo," replied the blue-eyed old man. "Mt. Asama is below us, and it's a natural formation. It does not bulge and expand as the station does."

"Mountains don't move?"

"That's right. There's even a saying. 'To be as still and unmoving as the natural mountain.'"

"Then the saying is wrong, sir. Because this one is," Nijo asserted, his eyes protruding extra hard. All of the white was visible around his irises, making them look like amphibian eggs.

Dr. Blue-Eyes exhaled through the nose and replied gravely, "Then it might be the precursor to an eruption."

Mt. Asama was an example of a stratovolcano, meaning it was a natural mountain formed by the layered buildup of multiple eruptions from the same vent over time.

There was a tendency in the station structure to form pie-crust layers of escalators and concrete over the stratovolcanoes found on Honshu. Some said this was a sign that the structural genetic field was incorporating geological information, too.

Mt. Fuji, the tallest of the natural mountains, underwent temporary shifts in its outer layers by the season, which were revered as Black Fuji and White Fuji by the locals. The station structure over Mt. Asama was not nearly so cyclical. It had a static mixture of white and black year-round that was known as pandagraph.

Dr. Blue-Eyes and the oddball young man with the protruding eyes lived in a town on the northern slope of Mt. Asama. The settlement did not have a real name, but folks referred to it as Hill Town.

If you traveled farther north, you would pass through a region called Tsumagoi, which led to big cities like Maebashi and Takasaki. The way to the west was covered in mountains, so there were plenty of people coming and going on the escalators.

"An eruption," Nijo began, lifting his hands up from below, "is when a natural mountain goes *herrupt!*, right? I read about it in a book. Is it really that common, though?"

"There hasn't been one since the mountain was Stationized, at the very least. And I've never heard of a volcano going off underneath the station structure."

"If someone as long-lived as you hasn't even heard of it happening before, it must be *extremely* rare. We are fortunate to get to witness it up close."

"Don't be morbid." Dr. Blue-Eyes glared at the younger man. In this era of escalators on all the slopes, foot traffic on the peaks was high. If an eruption happened now, casualties would be massive and unavoidable.

However, without knowing when the event might occur, any rash action might lead to panic. Because human travel Inside was limited by the size and range of the escalators, a rush of movement prompted by uncertain information could lead to calamity on its own.

"Maybe we should try to counteract it somehow with that strange tech you've got. Is that possible?"

"Well, sir, all I can do is interfere with Suikanet's functions. It's just a little tweak of the information on the net. It certainly can't do anything about the eruption of a natural mountain beneath us."

"I'm not asking you to do that. What I mean is that you could issue an evacuation through the system and try to keep people away from the area, that's all."

Nijo closed his large eyes and shook his head around while thinking. "Hmm. Well, I've never controlled nodes over such a wide area before. It would take some time. I can't say anything until I've tried…but if that's what you want, Dr. Blue-Eyes, I would certainly bend over backward to make it happen, as your eternal apprentice and follower."

Blue-Eyes had never once declared the man his apprentice.

Nijo's Suikanet interference was some kind of tweaking of the network placed all throughout the Inside world of Yokohama Station. As best as Blue-Eyes understood, it extracted and sent information while also manipulating outcomes.

For some reason, Nijo claimed this tech was something he'd learned "because of you, Doctor." Of course, the elderly man knew little about advanced stuff like that. He was just a medical professional, and although he used the network often for his work, his comprehension of computers was not much better than the average Insider's.

However, by talking to this vociferous young man, Blue-Eyes had started to understand the basics.

"Look, you know that animated program they're always broadcasting these days."

"Ahh, *Mr. Shyumai*. Yes, I've watched it. That's a really good program. It's going to wind up as compulsory education one day. You should really watch it, sir. Suikanet communications spread through majority rule, so when a lot of people want to see a show, it spreads around. It's impressive how much that series has grown," Nijo commented, but Dr. Blue-Eyes did not seem interested in the content of his statement.

"Maybe we could hijack its slot and send some kind of message instead," he suggested.

Nijo made a bitter face. "In this region, I might be able to do that with a lot of effort, but it would only be once in an entire week, which isn't a great way to get out an emergency evacuation order. We should seek a more direct method," he replied, opening a map on his laptop. "The Suikanet nodes under my control right now are the ones from here to here. I can also send one-to-one messages outside of this range. However, I can only establish real-time communication, intercept others' messages, and broadcast something to everyone within this scope."

The area on the map he indicated covered almost all of Hill Town. At some point, the man had gained mastery of the village's routes of transmissions. Dr. Blue-Eyes thought back on the recent past, wondering if he'd sent any messages he didn't want anyone else to see, but he couldn't remember anything other than contact with his patients.

"The heaviest traffic is on the west side of the mountain, so I'd like to cover that zone, if possible," he said.

"Due to its structure, Suikanet nodes are harder to obtain the farther away they are geographically."

"Then we'll actually have to go to the western slope to do it, I suppose."

"That's an extremely analog method, but since we're in a hurry, it'll have to do. I can only hope my skill in this discipline will increase in the future," said Nijo.

With that decided, the men were quick to get started. Dr. Blue-Eyes packed his usual supply bag with necessities. Meanwhile, Nijo returned to his room nearby and gathered up his laptop, a charger, and several devices and cables. The doctor put up a piece of paper on the back of the bookcase facing the hallway.

Clinic closed due to emergency. Please be wary of Mt. Asama. If there is any activity, evacuate far away from the mountain. ES

"Doctor, Doctor, what is that 'ES' at the end?"

"It's short for Eddie Shimazaki. Among gaijin, there was once a custom of signing one's name using shorthand."

Nijo bobbed his head with great interest.

"I'm ashamed to say that this is the first time I've heard your name."

"I don't think anyone's called me by it in the last ten years."

Not since my wife died, he thought.

2

Everyone who knew him just called him Dr. Blue-Eyes. This was because he was a doctor who possessed a very rare characteristic, among Insiders at least—blue eyes. They were a sign that he had gaijin blood.

Gaijin was a word that meant "outside person," so, in its literal sense, you would imagine it referred to people born outside of Yokohama Station. Dr. Blue-Eyes himself had thought as much up to a certain point in his life. But in truth, the term had a connotation that predated the life of Yokohama Station. It was a word reserved for people beyond a "national border" determined by geographic features or otherwise agreed upon by two groups.

Out of all the gaijin, his eponymous blue eyes were apparently a feature particularly associated with a group called Caucasians.

"Caucasians. Where did the people by this name live, I wonder?" pondered Nijo, the young man with bulging eyes. It was just after the fellow showed up in Gunma.

"I've heard it was far to the north."

"Perhaps it was Aomori. That means 'Blue Forest,' after all. Or perhaps from outside the station. In Hokkaido?"

"I don't know. Farther north, though," Dr. Blue-Eyes replied. He'd had this conversation dozens of times before in his life, but he wasn't especially interested in this part of his personal background.

"There are places beyond Hokkaido? What a world we live in! Perhaps there are red-eyed people found to the south, then. What do you think, Doctor?" Nijo pressed.

Blue-Eyes shook his head. "The reason people have black eyes to begin with is that they evolved under solar light."

He pulled a book of anatomy off the shelf and showed Nijo a cross section of an eyeball. Most of his collection was made of printed volumes. Few people Inside had such things. Printed books like these hardly existed within the station. He'd inherited the collection from his father.

"This is the structure of the eyeball. Nearly all people's irises—the colored part here—are black. This is what shuts out the light."

"Eyeballs shut out light? Wouldn't that be completely backward, Doctor?"

"That's how strong sunlight was. People who lived under the sun all the time developed dark eyes to limit the power of the light. Caucasians lived farther to the north, so the sunlight was weaker, and their eyes turned blue."

"Do you suppose Insiders will eventually gain blue eyes like yours, Doctor?"

"It's possible."

"In that case, you are an example of an evolved Insider. That's very special, Doctor!" Nijo declared, and he clapped his hands.

"Pipe down. You'll bother the neighbors." Dr. Blue-Eyes glanced toward the hallway.

Nijo lowered his tone of voice, but only a little. "Oops, my apologies. If I keep this up, you're going to evolve your ears to block out sound, too."

"That will not happen. Evolution comes about as the generations change. Individuals who are poorly adapted die earlier, and the stronger survive longer. This is how we evolve over time."

The doctor lifted his cup of coffee, his blue eyes peering somewhere into the distance. He couldn't see very far, of course; the closest object in that direction was the wall of the room past the bookcases.

His so-called Caucasian blood was from several generations ago, and the genetic traces were almost entirely gone. If he simply closed his distinctive blue eyes, his face was utterly Japanese in appearance.

His hair was still thick after sixty, but it had not a drop of melanin left and was as white as the station structure while it was forming. There were deep wrinkles in his face that spoke to the troubles of the life he'd led, but beyond that, his features were pleasing, and it was clear that he'd been handsome in his prime. This was why the striking color of his eyes seemed to disrupt the harmony of his appearance so fiercely.

People called him Dr. Blue-Eyes as a respectful nickname these days, because of his social status as a practitioner of medicine. When he was a boy, however, the name Blue-Eyes seemed like a stain, a foreign impurity that had invaded his genes. In fact, he did have vague memories of being discriminated against.

At that time, Yokohama Station did not yet cover all of Honshu; the northern boundary line was around Iwate. People debated what would happen when it reached the strait. Would it make landfall in Hokkaido? How would JR North Japan react? He recalled that there had been a scholar who spoke about genetic homogeneity due to geographic isolation.

If the station stopped human beings from moving about as much, there would be reduced genetic exchange. Local communities would lose diversity over time, until they were all homogenized, apparently.

Hearing that discussion made him feel as though his blue eyes were merely pollution, a bit of grit in the flattening of the genetic background.

"As generations change, eh?" Nijo repeated.

"Yes. Not that I'll have any part in that. I used to be married, though, until about a decade ago." Dr. Blue-Eyes pointed at a plastic photo stand on the farthest bookcase. The faded photograph was of a woman aged around forty.

"Ahh. I have a daughter back home, about seven," said Nijo, which almost caused the doctor to spit out the coffee he lifted to his lips. "What's the matter, Doctor?" he questioned. "When I said seven, I meant seven years old, not seven daughters. I don't have that kind of Suika money."

"I know that. You left a seven-year-old daughter behind to come to this forsaken place?"

"Now, you don't really mean that, Doctor. You've said that this is a tranquil and pleasant place to live."

"What exactly do you think a father's responsibility is?"

"What do you think it is, Doctor?"

He didn't have an answer for that.

"I fulfilled my primary parental obligation, which was arranging for her Suika implant. There is a saying back in Kyoto. Um, 'A child doesn't need a parent, something-something-something.'"

"You mean, 'A child doesn't need a parent to grow, but a Suika'?"

"Oh, so they say that one here, too? I suppose Yokohama Station *does* have a homogenous culture!" Nijo exclaimed, his large eyes rolling with wonder.

Dr. Blue-Eyes exhaled. It was rare for him to get so tired from speaking with a person. The man had come here from a city named Kyoto, far to the west, and it suddenly occurred to the doctor that while people raised in distant areas might speak the same language, they could possibly approach conversations in an entirely different way.

At any rate, Nijo's ability to interface with Suikanet was unquestionable.

Because Suikanet expanded automatically and organically as the station did, very little was known about its finer workings. It was all people could do to use the devices that grew from the station to contact one another. Until recently, Dr. Blue-Eyes had to walk to a kiosk several minutes away from his home to correspond with patients.

But then Nijo had come along and said, "If you just register with Suika, you could access Suikanet from your home computer, Doctor!"

Nijo set it all up himself. It made Dr. Blue-Eyes's work dramatically more efficient.

Because of that, the doctor trusted the young man (in terms of technology, not personality). That was why, when he brought his findings about Suikanet and suspected the mountain was moving, the doctor took him at his word and presumed it was the prelude to an eruption.

3

Traffic was heavy on the west side of Mt. Asama. An unbroken line of people went up the station-generated escalators, like pilgrims on a journey to a holy peak. Signs here and there said DON'T WALK ON THE

ESCALATORS, but in nearly all cases, the right side was kept open for those who wanted to walk faster.

Every now and then, automated turnstiles traveled on escalators. They were nearly twice as wide as a person and would block the escalator, forcing the movement behind them to stop. In that case, there would be two parallel rows of people behind them.

Dr. Blue-Eyes and Nijo were side by side in just such a queue, proceeding toward the peak of Mt. Asama. There was a turnstile four steps ahead of them. It swiveled its flat face, observing the surroundings.

Now that escalators had developed into the primary mode of transportation in Yokohama Station, there were more and more small cities forming on the mountainsides in Nagano. The west slope of Mt. Asama was one of the leading travel routes connecting these cities to the Kanto Plain. If you took the escalator up to the peak, then rode the proper one down toward your destination, it would carry you the whole way.

"I'm an outsider here in Gunma. If I'm doing anything funny on my own, the employees will be suspicious of me. But together with you, a respected doctor in the community, I enjoy a much greater degree of freedom," Nijo had suggested, which was why Dr. Blue-Eyes had accompanied him. Yet among the crowds, plenty of people looked just as weird as the young man. He probably would have been just fine alone, assuming he didn't act too conspicuously.

But here they were. Nijo clutched his container, looking around at the terrain with his alarmingly large eyes. Just as a doctor knew which organ was where inside the human body, Nijo seemed capable of spotting what he called Suikanet nodes. To Dr. Blue-Eyes, the field of escalators around here was just a black river, its flow disordered and haphazard.

There were brief landings here and there to manage the angle of the slope. Salespeople set up their shops there with station lunches and other necessities, sitting around and looking bored. Some station employees were also present, looking for unauthorized sellers to yell at. Some of the merchants also had to pick up their goods and evacuate when the bulky turnstiles came shoving through.

"If we're going to prepare for an eruption, we'll need to seal off this route, of course," whispered the doctor.

"That's right. I was just thinking of how we might do that. The best would be to use the automated turnstiles to shut it down, but that's a bit beyond my means at the moment. Instead, I could use Suikanet to change the display on the lightboards..."

Nijo spoke in a loud and clear voice, drawing funny looks from other people within earshot. One middle-aged woman noticed Dr. Blue-Eyes standing next to him and bowed her head. He returned the gesture, assuming she was a patient he'd aided in the past.

The turnstile a few steps ahead continued to do nothing more than swivel its head. Either it had no interest in their conversation or did not understand it. The doctor almost wondered if all its rotating would pull a screw loose, leaving its head to fall to the ground.

The closer the escalator got to the peak, the more spots there were with no roof. That was the black part of the pandagraph. The sky was overcast with no blue, but there wasn't any rain for now. Precipitation would block off all traffic in the area, forcing them to make a significant detour.

Even among the Insiders who lived around them, the question of whether the automated turnstiles understood human speech or not was a significant mystery. They could speak in a woman's voice, but it was all prerecorded lines.

If a human being violated Inside rules, they'd receive a Suika violation notice and be ejected from the station. That was the extent of the turnstiles' activity, so perhaps they did not need to comprehend speech to do their job.

However, the rules were not necessarily crystal clear. For example, there was one that prohibited violence against a resident of the station under threat of expulsion. The line that separated violence from nonviolence was unclear, though. No systematic studies had ever been conducted on it.

Some schools taught their pupils, "The automated turnstiles keep a record of everyone who doesn't listen to their parents or teachers." It might not have been true, but it was effective at setting a child straight.

Some religious types preached, "All your deeds are recorded on the

Suika. When a man dies, his record is judged by the turnstile of the afterlife, which sends him to Heaven or Hell." Dr. Blue-Eyes thought this was an effective way to increase one's devout followers.

"I can tell you that it does record positional information," Nijo stated. They were taking a break near the peak, eating their lunches in a spot with a view of the outside.

Near the top of Mt. Asama, little hills like this one were often left exposed to natural ground, creating tiny station hollows. The mountain seemed no different than usual at this point.

"More specifically, it keeps an accumulated history of positional data in Suikanet, which can be accessed by scanning your Suika. It's quite easy to do; even you could manage if I taught you."

"I had no idea."

"Many details of how the Suika works are unknown still. We have no surviving manuals."

"Manuals?" the doctor parroted while eating a steamed bun. "They have those?"

"It's rumored they existed in the early days. Humans at least partially designed the Suika, after all."

"Well, I knew that."

There had never been a manual to the human body in medical history. Everything people knew about medical science came from dissection and examination.

"This is what my locational history is like. Want to see?" said Nijo, entering a few commands into the black screen of his device. A window appeared displaying a map of the entire island of Honshu. "This is the complete record of my travel from the moment I got a Suika implant. So, about twenty years."

A green line appeared on the map. Nijo had been born in the center of Kyoto, and most of his childhood movement was around the Kansai region and Chugoku to the west of it. After age twenty, he settled in Kyoto for a while, until recently (probably when his daughter turned six) he headed to the east and arrived in Gunma.

"Looks like you've been all over the place."

"Going to Okayama when I was young was a good learning experience. The structure around the Great Seto Bridge is very fine and new, making it easier to spot the Suikanet nodes. It's much simpler to do stuff with them when they're exposed," Nijo explained, rotating the screen and handing it to the doctor. "Let's check out yours, too. Tap here and certify your Suika, then enter the following commands."

He typed on the keys as instructed, but the window did not display a map of Japan. It was only a mountain range, crossed with topographic contours. Although his life was three times as long as Nijo's, the scale of his map was not even a tenth as large.

"Whoo! Your range of travel is *pretty* narrow, Doctor," Nijo remarked, smirking obnoxiously.

The doctor had almost never left the Gunma area. Just circling Mt. Asama like this was a considerable travel chapter in his life. Part of that was because his profession made it impossible to leave home for very long. However, he also bore no incredible interest in visiting a different area of the world—the singular structure known as Yokohama Station.

Some people might find journeying interesting, but being a famous person meant that others came to him. He didn't need to walk to anywhere else.

It was one year ago that the bug-eyed Nijo had come to Gunma.

With as much traffic as Mt. Asama got, outsiders spending a long time in the area was not a rare occurrence. Many people even came following the rumors of a man with mysterious blue eyes.

What made Nijo different, however, was that he didn't come to see Dr. Blue-Eyes for his strange appearance or for his skill as a doctor, but instead, for his language knowledge.

4

Different regions within Yokohama Station generated their own identification signs, which contained multiple text types. Ordinarily, it would have the name of the location written in kanji, with smaller alphabetical letters below that, so that they looked like this:

前橋 MAEBASHI

高崎 TAKASAKI

太田 OTA

By carefully examining the letters on a few of these signs, it was eventually possible to discern that there were about twenty-four or so of those letters, and that they suggested the pronunciation of the place's name. It started with the vowel sound of *a*, and eventually, you had a list of the whole alphabet.

Furthermore, when you saw a sign like 前橋 MAEBASHI, there was bound to be another sign farther away that said 前橋方面 FOR MAEBASHI.

Logically, this would suggest that the letters *for* corresponded to 方面, meaning "the direction of." The problem was that, unlike the place names, this word did not relate to any proper use of Japanese that anyone knew of. There was no sound scribed to the letters *fo*, and no solitary *r* without a vowel sound of its own in Japanese. On top of that, the mysterious word preceded MAEBASHI rather than following it, as it would in proper Japanese.

At this point, a clever person would recognize that the location signs Inside generated actually contained two different languages entirely. The problem was that there was very little you could do after that. There were almost no reference materials to consult.

"They're in a language called English," Dr. Blue-Eyes explained. This happened on the very first day the bug-eyed, fast-speaking young man arrived from the west side of Mt. Asama.

"Caucasians used this language, from what I understand. *For* is something called a preposition, and it has many meanings, not just 'direction.' You have to discern which meaning it is through context."

"Ahh, ahh!" Nijo marveled, jotting down notes on his laptop.

There were several English books in Dr. Blue-Eyes's library. Some were dictionaries and other reference texts about using the language, while others were simply written in English. The majority were faded and discolored. A few were so degraded that it was difficult to turn their pages.

Using what his mother taught him, Dr. Blue-Eyes read them for intellectual stimulation when he wasn't busy with work.

"Uh, so just to sum this up, your father had Caucasian blood, and your mother taught you English?"

"That's right. My father died quite young, so I have no memory of him speaking it."

Nijo made a truly bemused face. "But earlier, you said that English was the language of the Caucasians."

"Right."

"So does that mean language is not determined by genetics?"

"…?"

"I had heard that people in the past spoke different languages depending on the region. I suppose that isn't an effect of their genes, then."

"Well, of course not. Words are things we learn as we grow. A Japanese person raised in a place where Japanese isn't spoken is going to learn the local dialect instead."

"I see. The veil has been lifted from my eyes," Nijo said delightedly. "If the station structure has learned this English, would that not suggest that in Japan before the station expanded, Japanese and the language of the Caucasians coexisted in some form?"

"Perhaps that's true."

"Then maybe the relative size of the letters is meant to indicate the ratio of the races among the population? But I must admit that I've hardly ever seen anyone with Caucasian blood like you, Doctor. Where did they go, I wonder?"

"Dunno," answered Dr. Blue-Eyes.

Before Yokohama Station covered all of Honshu, there had allegedly been a long war, but very little was known about it. Several countries used satellite weaponry and combat robots, invading one another's territories and leading to occupying forces and endless refugees. The conflict had been inescapable.

"Anyway, I now understand that *for* is a preposition. But what do these words mean, Doctor?"

Nijo showed him the screen of his laptop. There was a green text string on a black background.

```
FOR (HEADER IN PURGEDHEADERS) {
PREPAREDREQUEST.HEADERS.POP(HEADER)
}
```

"What is this?" questioned Dr. Blue-Eyes, his brow wrinkling. "For one thing, English sentences don't use this kind of punctuation. Or they do, but not in this way."

"Then is it possible that this is some third language, not the ones Caucasians speak?"

"What is this writing?"

"That's what I was hoping to find out," replied Nijo. He scrolled upward. The very top line read:

```
#!/USR/BIN/ENV CODAMA
```

"I found this text on Suikanet. Years ago, around the Great Seto Bridge, I found—oh, the Great Seto Bridge is a large passage far to the west, even farther than Kyoto. Anyway, I found a place where the network nodes were exposed and easy to scoop out. If my thinking is correct, this is the language that governs Suikanet. If we can decode this, I'm certain we'll be able to control the network's communications, and perhaps even the actions of the automated turnstiles."

Another eccentric, thought Dr. Blue-Eyes.

It seemed he was due to receive a visit from some oddball engineer roughly once a year. Every one of them would say, "I've got this wonderful"—(in his opinion)—"invention, and I want your help in spreading it to the world." As a local famous figure and doctor, they seemed to think that his Suika was simply bursting with funds.

Nijo, however, did not bring up the topic of money at all. He was more curious about the meaning of the esoteric writing.

"What do you suppose *class* means?"

"A school year, or a lecture session."

"I see. So would *class Connection* mean something like 'friendship among schoolmates,' perhaps? Next question: What is *import?*"

"It means to purchase supplies from a foreign country and bring them into your own."

"Maybe this text comes from a time when there was trade with foreign nations. I mean, it stands to reason, being written in this foreign language."

With each uncertain answer Dr. Blue-Eyes gave, Nijo arrived at his own interpretation of the sentence. The doctor didn't feel his knowledge was actually helping in any way, but the young man wasn't bothered in the least by the process.

Eventually, a regular patient came by for a scheduled visit, so the doctor pulled down a dictionary (the easiest to read) and handed it to Nijo.

"Look up the rest on your own. It's a family heirloom, so I can't give it to you, but I don't mind you consulting it here. Give it back when you're done deciphering those bizarre messages."

"You mean it?" Nijo asked, his already prominent eyes protruding even further. He bowed deeply.

Dr. Blue-Eyes's error was in not realizing that Nijo's mysterious text was actually thousands upon thousands of lines, and that decoding them would keep him in Hill Town for an indefinite length of time.

Nijo ended up staying in the cramped, recently built storeroom next to Dr. Blue-Eyes's place. It had a metal door that had started out rusted, and it was damp and extremely dark, which made it unsuited even for storage space. He didn't have any other use for it.

Usually, the young man worked alone, muttering to himself at all hours of the day and night, with the occasional outburst like "I've got it! I've figured it out!" or "This is truly confounding" or "The segmentation has faulted again. Well, now I'm at an impasse."

Dr. Blue-Eyes's home was also his office, so sometimes, he got complaints from the patients resting on the bed there, saying, "I can hear a voice behind the wall that sounds like the muttering of the dead." The culprit was most certainly alive, and Dr. Blue-Eyes mused that Nijo was capable of causing much more trouble than the dead could ever dream of.

5

Mt. Asama was covered in station all the way to the peak. Aside from the tiny hollows created by the undulations in the ground there, it was a model example of a stratovolcano within Yokohama Station.

The mouth, five hundred meters across, was ringed by hallways, which offered a foothold to stack more floors upon until it covered the top of the volcano in a dome, like a particularly aerated wicker basket. Because the corridors were not airtight, they were constantly full of the stench of hydrogen sulfide.

If Yokohama Station completely blocked the mouth of the volcano, the pressure inside would build until it caused a steam explosion. The structure seemed to understand this, because it had constructed a cage-like system that allowed the pressure to escape.

There were no tourists here. Mt. Asama was a travel route, so very few people went out of their way to visit the caldera. At some point, someone had decided to sort the mountains of Japan into two mutually exclusive purposes: travel or sightseeing.

"First, let's set up a fixed interference antenna here."

Nijo removed a terminal about the size of his palm from his bag, looked around for a plug underfoot, and stuck the charging cable in. The device beeped, and its screen turned on, displaying a message that said it was booting up. Then he retrieved his laptop and entered a few commands with a rapid but steady rhythm. The smaller device's screen now stated that its setup was complete.

"If we figure out the curvature of the dome, we should be able to measure the internal pressure to a certain degree. If this thing keeps emitting jamming signals, it will control the Suikanet nodes around this spot the way I command it to."

"Hmm. Like a handicap stone."

"Handicap stone?"

"You don't play *Go*? They're pieces that a beginner gets to have on the board at the start of a game against an experienced player. By having them down at the start, it makes it easier to capture the territory around them," Dr. Blue-Eyes explained.

Nijo nodded with delight. "Ahh, what a clever analogy. Brilliant, Doctor! Then let us call this our handicap stone," he said.

He pulled out a piece of paper, scrawled a message on it in pen, and placed it under the "stone."

In place for surveying purposes. Please do not touch. K2

"What's with the K2?"

"Those are *my* initials. Keijin Nijo, K2."

Dr. Blue-Eyes chose not to tell him that he wouldn't use *2* for *Ni*, but the English letter *N*.

"I'm not sure if that's going to be as effective as you want. Do this instead," he suggested while producing a red pen and a fresh sheet of paper.

This device was generated by the station on this spot. Removing it will be seen as destruction of station material and might cause your Suika to be invalidated.

"Oooh! Excellent, sir. Nobody will want to touch it now. Not only are you a medical expert, but you are also extremely cunning."

"It's not my idea. I saw the same thing done before, ages ago. The older, the wiser, that's all."

"I see, I see!" Nijo was positively beaming.

Of course, everyone who lived Inside understood that nothing you could accomplish with human hands rose to the level of "destruction of station material." But now that there was a written warning, nobody was going to risk it.

With that step complete, the two descended an elevator to the southwest. There were five devices they had that could be placed as handicap stones. The village was on the north slope, so the most effective strategy was to put one on the peak and a number along the southern side.

The south slope was quite lonely. The only sounds were the humming of the escalators and the thunking of the automated turnstiles' footsteps. Occasionally, there was a distant *gashunk, galank, galunk, galank* noise. The pair discerned that it happened every fifteen minutes by checking the clock.

"You don't suppose the eruption's started already, do you?" Nijo questioned. Despite the serious nature of the inquiry, his face suggested a hint of glee.

"I've never heard an eruption, so I couldn't say...but if you asked me, it resembles a machine more than rocks crumbling."

"That's a good point. Perhaps there's a scrapyard nearby."

"I came this way for a patient visit about three years ago and didn't see anything like that," replied Dr. Blue-Eyes.

A scrapyard was a turnstile disposal facility. Automated turnstiles that were past their service life went to such places to be dismantled by other turnstiles. The facilities weren't massive places, but the doctor thought it was unlikely one would grow here in the mountains after only a few years.

Unlike the west slope of Mt. Asama, which was a main travel thoroughfare, there was almost no one on the south slope. It wasn't the shortest route between any two cities. The station structure had a tendency to generate features where it detected the most foot traffic, so the hallways here were shabby. There were gaps in the escalator slopes, and many of them weren't moving. Perhaps the electrical systems were breaking down. That was only going to drive more people away. The process of reshaping the hallways was known as colony optimization.

But that didn't mean this region of the mountain was utterly empty and still. While there were no settlements, automated turnstiles could be seen anywhere in Yokohama Station. Some stood unmoving on landings, while others just circled endlessly, going up and down the escalators.

"For there being no people here, the turnstiles certainly seem quite busy, Doctor," Nijo noted.

"It wasn't like this three years ago, as I recall. There weren't any people then, either, but all the turnstiles were stopped, for the most part."

"Perhaps this is another harbinger of eruption. It's quite a fascinating phenomenon, if so." The younger man smirked. Books mentioned that birds and other animals would flee when an eruption was imminent on natural mountains. Some believed that wild animals possessed instincts that civilization had taken away from people.

Gashunk, galank, galunk, galank.

As the two headed along the mountainside toward the spot for their next handicap stone, it seemed as though the strange mechanical sounds were getting closer.

When they were stationary and seen from a distance, there was no major difference between humans and turnstiles, but the disparity couldn't be more obvious when the machines were walking.

When humans climbed the narrow escalators, they waited to see if the person in front had moved before taking the next step. That created a split-second lag between each individual.

The automated turnstiles had no such gap, however. Surely, there was some level of individual difference depending on how well their electrical systems and motors were functioning, but it wasn't enough that a human being could detect it. So when there was a line of multiple turnstiles in a row, they seemed to march upward in unison, like one machine.

"Oh! Doctor, look over there!" Nijo cried, pointing down the slope at a highly bizarre escalator. A silver lane stuck out of the mountainside almost vertically, pointing into empty space. From a distance, it looked like a chainsaw stuck into the slope.

At the end was a group of about four turnstiles, stock-still. Display boards were affixed to their narrow necks, but they were facing the other way, so it was impossible to see what they were displaying.

Eventually, a fifth turnstile rose up the escalator from the next landing down. When it reached the top, the quartet took one step forward, pushed by the new one. The turnstile in the lead stepped out onto thin air and fell off the landing.

As it descended, spinning, its face was visible briefly. As always, it showed a white smiling face on a black background.

It collapsed onto a linoleum floor plastered to the mountainside. It landed with a heavy *gashunk*, then tumbled into the valley, *galank, galunk, galank*.

"Did you see that, Doctor? What a sight!" Nijo chuckled, very excited.

"What are they doing? Suicide by jumping?"

"That's probably a fault of their movement programming. They're designed to maintain a certain distance from one another and never go the wrong direction on escalators. So when five of them jam up in a narrow space, one is going to be pushed off and fall. How fascinating!" Nijo shouted. "Now that we've solved that mystery, let's continue. The spot for our next stone is very close."

Multiple automated turnstiles were milling about at the base of the bizarre escalator. Exactly every fifteen minutes, one of them would climb onto the escalator and eventually push off another one.

A vast pile of immobile turnstiles was at the bottom of the slope, their limbs broken and twisted. Other turnstiles were gathering around the mound and picking up the pieces, carrying them off somewhere else. Apparently, they even had a routine to perform when they discovered a destroyed turnstile.

Programmed suicide.

Just contemplating the concept started making Dr. Blue-Eyes sick to his stomach, and he had to sit down on the escalator.

"Doctor? What's the matter? Need a break?"

"Be quiet for a little, Nijo."

"Very well. I will stop talking. You deserve a rest from all the walking, sir," Nijo agreed, in what passed for hushed tones by his standards. They let the escalator carry them toward their next destination.

The only sounds on the lonely slope were straightforward and repetitious. The footsteps of automated turnstiles, the hum of the escalators, and the PA announcing, **"Please hold on to the handrail and stay inside the yellow line."** To every Insider, these had been heard since birth and were merely background noise. You learned to filter them out of your head, like the ticking of a clock.

When the din was erased from the mind, one thing remained that could not be ignored.

"Someone's talking," muttered Dr. Blue-Eyes. "A human voice. There's a person nearby."

6

"Huh? That's a human voice?" Nijo asked.

Dr. Blue-Eyes pointed to an open door between escalators. "You don't hear it? Someone's whispering over there. Probably a woman."

"Oh, I hear it. I just thought it was a turnstile."

Now the doctor couldn't be so sure anymore. The words had a slightly different tone than the familiar sound of the automated turnstiles, which every person who lived Inside knew. However, it was also too flat and repetitive to be human.

After the door, the hallway passed under the escalators, proceeding level along the contour of the mountain. The voice was coming from farther down. They were close to the mouth of the volcano; if an eruption occurred, this area was sure to be filled with smoke.

Farther along, there were four automated turnstiles, facing outward. Two of the machines turned their heads when the men approached them.

"You are leaving the station. Please be aware that you will need a Suika to reenter."

They sidled against the wall to clear the path.

By definition, any place not consumed by the structure of Yokohama Station was "outside." It happened the most in the mountains, where undulations in the surface made the generation of the building impossible. These became highly isolated exterior spots, known as station hollows.

Yet for whatever reason, there were also spots the automated turnstiles labeled as outside despite being firmly within the complex. This seemed to be one of them.

"Wow, my first time outside in ages. It's physically within the building, so it looks the same—but the air always feels different beyond the boundaries," Nijo commented, marveling. Dr. Blue-Eyes could only grunt noncommittally.

"Have you ever left the station, Doctor?"

"A few times. When I need to perform special treatment. It's called an injection. I stick a small needle into a person's body in order to deliver some kind of medicinal solution into the bloodstream directly. Can't do that Inside, of course."

Nijo laughed. "A needle? To heal someone? It seems positively immoral."

The repetitive voice had stopped at some point, but the two continued walking. The hallway was curving gently with the contour of the mountain. The farther they went, the fewer lights there were, making it steadily darker. There was a pungent smell around them.

At the very end was a small, dark room. There was a couch in the corner with black cushions and something that looked like a white blanket resting atop it.

When Nijo approached the blanket, it made an animal sound like "Aaa, aauuu?" and rolled off the couch. It tumbled onto the exposed concrete floor and shrieked, then put its hands on the floor and stood.

It was not a comforter but a person. A girl of about eight or nine years, with unkempt hair so long that it reached the floor. When she saw Dr. Blue-Eyes and Nijo, she made another bestial "Aauaa," then began to smack the doctor around the waist with both hands.

"Were you the one making that sound?" Dr. Blue-Eyes asked.

"Aa?"

She looked at him, then used both hands to clench his thigh through his pants. She was fascinated, as though she'd never gotten the chance to examine a human body before.

"Is there anyone else around?" he continued, submitting to the physical examination of his leg.

"Eee, eee," the girl responded, and she pointed to the hallway they'd just come down.

"Doesn't seem like she understands language," Nijo remarked from the rear.

"Do you know your name? N-a-m-e," said the doctor. The pudgy girl made a gesture of understanding something, clapping her hands.

"Suika not detectid. Pleez present a vallid Suika or tikit to entir," she recited all at once. Unlike her animalistic grunts, this was as flat and monotonous as a machine. The men immediately recognized it as the words of the turnstiles.

"Ohhh... That solves it, Doctor. She's been cast out."

"So it would seem," answered Dr. Blue-Eyes, putting a hand to his forehead. "Her parents must not have been able to cover the cost of the Suika implant."

Nijo looked around the little room. It was too dark, so he pulled out his device and turned on the light, pointing it at some large trash receptacles in the corner.

"I think she must be getting stuff from there."

He went to the line of three trash cans and opened the lid on the one marked FLAMMABLE TRASH. It was connected to some other, much larger space, judging by the sound of rushing wind on the other side. Nijo stuck his arm inside and pulled out some sealed pieces of bread and a bento lunch.

"It's a cramped space, but she seems to have all she needs to survive. Which is how...*this* happened," he stated, glancing at the girl.

While Dr. Blue-Eyes attempted to communicate with the plump child, Nijo rifled around in the corners of the room and discovered a notebook stuck behind a white pipe close to the ceiling. It was marked with entries in red ink.

April 2: Two months have passed since coming here. I suppose it's fortunate that food is delivered to this place, but I'm not really sure. There is nothing to do but eat. Thankfully, there are multiple trash cans, so I can keep the flammable trash can with the food clean and use the empty can as a toilet. Food situation is good for now.

April 7: I'm so bored that I've started practicing my dropkicks against the automated turnstiles. Surprisingly, I can beat one of them, but I'm blocked by the other three and can't escape. After many tries, I messed up my knee, so that's the end of that.

April 15: I thought if I destroyed the top of the trash can, I might be able to get Inside, but it's impossible to harm with my bare hands. It must be fastened in place by several screws.

April 29: Found a piece of metal in the flammable trash. Think I might be able to use it as a screwdriver. Food situation: good.

April 30: Peeled off the paint and exposed the screwheads. I was worried this would count as destruction of station property, but then I chuckled when I realized I'd already been expelled from the station, so it doesn't matter. It's been a while since I had a good laugh."

April 30: Destroyed one screwhead. Trying to think of a better method. Food situation: good.

May 2: The broken screwhead is back to normal.

May 14: I don't know my current location, probably the south side of Mt. Asama. Virtually no one passes this way.

May 17: The only thing I think about anymore is where the trash can leads. I hope it's connected to somewhere spacious.

My clock battery is dead, so I can't tell the date anymore. Food situation: worrisome.

Why can't human beings eat food and store it for later?

The turnstiles brought a girl. Probably not for violations, but because she came of age.

The girl can hardly speak a word. A six-year-old should at least know how to say a few things. I suspect she was abandoned shortly after birth by her parents. Food situation: troubled.

If I get any skinnier, I might fit into the trash can without needing to take off the lid.

Would it have been any better closer to the ocean? But I've heard that people outside the station along the coasts have their own colonies, which is frightening in its own way. Food situation: perilous.

I can't go back Inside due to a Suika violation, but perhaps someone who wanders by here can help her acquire a Suika and allow her to get back Inside.

I'll leave this in a spot high up so that she doesn't accidentally throw it away.

That was where the entries ended.

"What should we do now, Doctor?" asked Nijo, giving Blue-Eyes a piercing look. The doctor averted his eyes.

"I know what you're asking," he replied. "I've seen a number of children like her, and those who could have turned out like her. If we go to a nearby town, drag back a bioelectric technician with us, and pay the five hundred thousand milliyen, we could free her from this cage. But we shouldn't."

"Ahh, we shouldn't?" Nijo questioned, pondering this statement. He smacked his fist into his palm. "I see! So what you're saying is, as a wealthy doctor, you have the means of giving this girl a Suika and getting her out of here. But if you do that, other parents with kids of their own will think that's unfair. *'Why did you save her and not our children?'* they'll ask. So you choose out of principle not to save any kids whatsoever."

"Nijo, I beg of you—stop talking," spat Dr. Blue-Eyes with a baleful glare. The younger man made a show of clamping his hands over his mouth.

The girl sensed something ominous in their conversation. She said, "Paa, paa," and pulled a bag of bakery snacks from under the couch, offering them to the doctor.

They headed back into the hallway, leaving her behind. The four turnstiles were lined up in a row, facing their direction. When the turnstiles saw them, the two in the middle sidled out of the way.

"Keijin Nijo, your Suika is confirmed. Thank you for visiting Yokohama Station."

"Eddie Shimazaki, your Suika is confirmed. Thank you for visiting Yokohama Station."

They spoke in the same voice, delivered at just a fraction of a second's differential, creating an ugly echo. It occurred to Dr. Blue-Eyes that these automated turnstiles were the only things that would refer to him by name anymore.

7

They made their way around the entire mountain, placing their handicap stones where appropriate, and returned to Hill Town two days after they'd left.

"That completes our placement of the stones. If anything happens, I'll be sure to let you know at once," said Nijo. He promptly holed himself up in the room next to Dr. Blue-Eyes's.

For a while after that, regular life persisted. The doctor continued his practice and spent his free time reading books and occasionally thinking about that fat little girl. The frequency of earthquakes dropped, and so did the strange exclamations that Nijo made next door.

Dr. Blue-Eyes began to wonder if this was all just Nijo getting ideas into his head. Obviously, the lack of an eruption was a *good* thing. However, Nijo already gave people a poor first impression, and the fact that he'd embarked on a two-day wild goose chase might worsen that reputation.

"We've had enough, Doctor," said a man who acted as a kind of town dignitary. He'd led off with a long speech about how much the town depended on the doctor to survive. "That bug-eyed man is leading you on. Please, from all of us, just kick him out and send him on his way."

"This town is along a traffic route, so anyone is free to settle down in any room they find," he snapped. That response was the spark that caused the locals' frustrations about Nijo to explode. Within a few days, there was a line of petitioners outside Dr. Blue-Eyes's office.

"I speak for a group of ascetics in the mountains," said a woman dressed in white, with the phrase *All things have the Station-nature* written in kanji on her sleeve. "Our training place is in a station hollow on the north face, where it is open to the sky. This way, we can purify our bodies with valuable natural rain." With that explanation out of the way, she continued, "Then that man barged in without warning, and he started blathering about how the surface tension made the density of Suikanet so high around station hollows."

Dr. Blue-Eyes could not envision what their training involved for the life of him, but she painted a very vivid picture of Nijo.

"Er, I hate to interrupt, but why does a man's presence interfere with your training?"

"The station's ability to replicate is rooted in its femininity. So if a man enters the sanctity of the training grounds, he introduces impure male essence," she claimed.

A man asserted that Nijo was intercepting private communications. But Dr. Blue-Eyes remembered that this person had come to Nijo before and gotten help with his technical trouble.

After several days of nonstop complaints, he could no longer get any reasonable amount of work done, so he went to knock on Nijo's door.

"Are you in there? I need to talk with you," he called, opening the door.

Nijo was seated, his eyes locked on his screen. "Dr. Blue-Eyes. The handicap stones on the mountain have vanished."

His voice was strangely quiet. Dr. Blue-Eyes marveled that he was capable of speaking so softly at all.

"Vanished? You mean the signals died out?"

"No, they've physically disappeared. However, the log shows a sudden surge in the temperature sensors just before they did." Nijo played a very grainy video on the screen. "Look, this is the final image captured by the rooftop camera."

Black smoke spilled from the top of the mountain with tremendous force, and within a few seconds, an ebony shape (most likely some volcanic rock) flew toward the lens, and then all was dark.

"Go ahead, Doctor," Nijo said, his voice oddly calm. He held out what seemed to be a speaker acting as a mic, its paper cone exposed. The controlled volume of his voice impressed upon the doctor the gravity of the situation.

"I have to do it?"

"Well, of course. If I made the announcement, it would only harm my already-poor standing. I don't have the space to save a recording, so we have to do it live. The camera's right there, so look in that direction. I'll hook us up in five seconds."

"Five seconds?"

He didn't even have time to be alarmed. Nijo started counting down on his fingers.

"Er, *ahem, ahem*." Dr. Blue-Eyes coughed. Voices from down the hallway yelped, "What's this?" and "Isn't that Dr. Blue-Eyes?"

"All residents in the Mt. Asama area. The mountain is currently erupting, putting us in a perilous situation. Use the downward escalators and evacuate to a place as far from the volcano caldera as you can. Uh, station employees, please offer guidance to the elderly and children to help them evacuate. I repeat. The mountain is currently…"

His words came out of the speakers in the hallway a second after he spoke them, creating a very odd echoing effect. On top of that, the sound of his voice was not at all the way he heard it from inside his head.

"Well done, Doctor. All that's left to do is whip up an evacuation route to show them. We should get moving, too."

"How far was that message just broadcast, exactly?"

"It got displayed on pretty much all the guidance boards that hang from the ceiling. And there are lots of spots that only have speakers, no monitors."

Somewhere in the distance, *thud*s and *slam*s sounded from the ceiling, as though there were objects falling from above. Apparently, a volcanic projectile had landed over their heads.

How many floors of the station are above us here? The doctor had been living in the area for a long while, so more levels must have grown in that time.

Nijo had already been gathering his possessions during the announcement, and he promptly picked them up and walked out of the room. Dr. Blue-Eyes followed him. On the way to the down escalator, he stopped at his own chamber, glanced at the piles of books on his bookcases, then picked up only the bag full of medical supplies and hurried out.

There was a huge line of people on the descending escalator.

"Dr. Blue-Eyes!"

"Was that really you on the announcement, Doctor?" someone demanded.

"Don't panic, please. Just focus on evacuating to safety for…"

Just then, there was another series of *bang*s and *boom*s. It was much closer than before. Perhaps the layers above them were thinner than he realized. A person screamed.

When they reached a more open space, they saw that the station's roof had already been punctured by heated rocks the size of automated turnstiles. The residents had never seen natural boulders in their lives and gazed at them with great curiosity. A few took pictures. Stones and ash fell through the holes in the ceiling.

As Yokohama Station developed and escalators became the primary mode of transportation, the population gravitated toward the mountains rather than the plains, especially compared to the era of human-built cities. Before the station's growth, hardly anyone would have ever attempted to live within the range of volcanic projectiles, surely.

"Seems like quite a few were too late to escape the slope," Nijo noted. He had his laptop open while standing on the escalator, and the map displayed on the screen showed red dots all over. The eruption had damaged Yokohama Station in many places, and people who'd lost their evacuation routes were wandering with nowhere to go.

"Each one of these dots is a person?"

From what he could see on the screen, over a hundred had been left behind.

"Yes. Although technically, they're Suika implants."

"And I suppose even the station employees can't go rescue them... Oh, why don't we use the automated turnstiles?"

"Huh?"

"You once told me that if you controlled Suikanet, you could manipulate the turnstiles. You were extremely proud of it, as I recall."

"Listen, that was more like a business pitch than anything. All I can do is overwrite a few variables and flag values. There's no way for me to reprogram them with anything complex like escorting people to safe...ty... *Oh!*"

"Did you remember something?"

"Well, I've never done it before, so this would be an attempt on the fly..."

While using one hand to prop up the laptop, he entered commands with the other.

"I'll reverse two flags on the automated turnstiles' action algorithm. They're the ones for Suika possession and movement direction. Normally, they attempt to push people without Suikas outside of the station, but if I switch them, they'll try to push people *with* Suikas *away* from the outside. Because the top of the mountain is blowing off and becoming outside, they should carry the people who failed to escape down to the foot of the mountain. In theory, at least."

And with that, Nijo smacked the ENTER key.

"It's the only thing we can do now. Let's try it," said the doctor.

"I've already executed the command. All we can do is pray."

After several hours of descent, they reached flat ground, where a huge crowd of evacuees was already gathered, clamoring and panicked. Dr. Blue-Eyes borrowed an infirmary and started aiding people there. By passing through areas without roofing during the evacuation, many had inhaled volcanic ash or fallen and hurt themselves.

As each person came through, they said, "It's him! The man from the broadcast!" Soon the hallway was packed with people. Every day, he was surrounded by a crowd of patients in need and other assorted onlookers. It was exhausting.

He gave instructions to bring together all of the medical practitioners in the surrounding area, then fell into a deep sleep for nearly two whole days.

When he woke again, there were posters of him put up all over Inside. Apparently, screenshots were taken of his evacuation transmission, and they were made into fliers.

Dr. Blue-Eyes is watching you. Follow the rules of Inside! said the large caption. Underneath, in smaller letters, it read, *To victims of the Mt. Asama eruption: For current medical information and emergency food supply, please see Yokohama Station West Gunma Region Employee Association, Skynet Address: XXXX-XXXX.*

That suggested it was local station employees who were issuing the posters. In the few days since the eruption, the station employees had presented *him* as their leader, presumably because they were desperate for someone to follow. Evidently, people who'd never met the doctor before saw in his blue eyes something greater, a transcending of their common humanity.

An article made the rounds on Suikanet titled "How Dr. Blue-Eyes, Physician of Hill Town, Anticipated the Eruption of Mt. Asama and Averted Disaster." Based on the inclusion of the handicap stones, Nijo himself had likely penned it. Information that was frequently viewed on Suikanet spread to more distant nodes. Thus, the article circulated until Dr. Blue-Eyes became something of a celebrity within Yokohama Station.

8

"Took a whole chunk of it, huh, Doctor?" asked the employee.

She was a young woman with a tendency to uptalk. She had to be

several years younger than Nijo, but it was hard to tell the subtle difference in younger people when you got to be the doctor's age.

"Hmm? Did you say something, Mugino?"

"I said, it took a whole chunk of the mountain out."

"Ah, pardon me," he said, dipping his head in apology. Unlike being
inside Yokohama Station, there was no echo up on the roof, so it was
harder to make out voices, even at close range. Perhaps being around
that loudmouth Nijo for so long had made him a bit hard of hearing.

"I suppose that's why they're calling it a sector collapse," he remarked,
holding his hand up and squinting to block the sun.

Judging by the view from the rooftops over Tsumagoi, the northern
part of Mt. Asama was simply gone, as though scooped away by a giant
spoon. Even from a distance, they could see rubble from the collapse of
the station structure within the gouged side of the mountain, its sil-
houette jagged and ugly. The natural peak was like a symbol of the
immovable. And faced with such a dynamic shift in its presentation,
Dr. Blue-Eyes had to wonder just what the difference was between the
station and the natural landscape anyway.

The roiling smoke had finally dissipated, and there was now a layer
of ash several centimeters thick atop Yokohama Station. However, the
sky was a piercing blue color. There were no seasons Inside, so it was
hard for them to know if it was spring or autumn, just that the temperature was pleasant.

Dr. Blue-Eyes, however, was not enamored with the azure expanse
overhead. Going onto the roof when the sun was out was so painful
that he could hardly open his eyes. Few other Insiders seemed to have
this weakness, so perhaps something was wrong with him.

"Doctor, was your house around there?" Mugino asked, pointing
toward the collapse.

"I can't tell from this angle, but most likely."

"Wow... Rest in peace," the young woman said sadly. The library
he'd inherited from his father was probably buried somewhere within
that heap. The printed books had been made during the war; his father
said he'd inherited them from *his* father. Now that legacy was ash, just

like the bloodline that would end with the doctor, for not having any progeny of his own.

Later, Dr. Blue-Eyes was made a local leader due to his prediction of the eruption and subsequent evacuation of the residents. Station employees also assigned Mugino, a young staffer, to be his assistant. This gave them a means of seeking the wisdom of their leader (or, more accurately, getting his approval of their plans).

Because the people of Hill Town had evacuated to the mountain base, there was a shortage of supplies, from food to medical care. What's more, because the slope was impassable now, the route of human travel had to change considerably, sending vast numbers of people through places that had previously been ignored.

Naturally, that caused all kinds of trouble, which required the intervention of the station employees. Yet when critical decisions needed to be made, they looked to Dr. Blue-Eyes for mediation. In other words, residents accepted rulings more readily when his name was used, making things far less troublesome.

"I'm still young, so I don't know what it was like when we had a human government," Mugino stated. Neither did Dr. Blue-Eyes, but he let the comment slide. "I feel like, having a leader with a face you can see? That's necessary for times like this. Especially in a disaster, it makes people feel at ease to see an old man who looks kind and smart like you, who can tell people that things will be all right."

"I see," the doctor replied. He appreciated the sentiment, of course. But he felt better suited to seeing patients in his clinic one by one rather than speaking to an entire crowd of thousands and hearing nothing in return. "Do we have a total number of casualties, then?"

"Yes. Judging by our citizenship records, we've got fifty-two dead and two hundred and eighty-eight wounded. The authorities are saying it's miraculously low for the scale of destruction? Almost all of the dead were living on the north side, but there are many comments from survivors who say automated turnstiles brought them down the mountain," she explained, without even looking at the device in her hands.

The airheaded way of speaking Mugino employed belied a rather sharp mind.

They had their own registry of the citizenry, separate from Suika registration, and because it was managed by people, it was more useful than Suika in scenarios like these. Especially without excellent Suika-net technicians like Nijo.

Still, Dr. Blue-Eyes couldn't for the life of him understand their basis for saying the damages were "miraculously low." No other natural disasters had occurred on this scale Inside, so there couldn't possibly be anything to compare it to.

"It seems like marshaling the automated turnstiles worked like a charm, Nijo. Very well done," praised Dr. Blue-Eyes.

"To be honest, I'd say it was more like half-well done, sir. Not in terms of the number of people saved, I mean, but in terms of the number of automated turnstiles," Nijo responded. "Inverting the control flags only works to a certain probability. It was the variables for Suika presence and the direction to push people. If you flip both of them, they take people with Suika to safety at the foot of the mountain, but there were a high number of them who only inverted one of the two variables."

"So what happened with them?"

"They kicked people with Suika implants out of the station. In this case, since the eruption had just blown part of the station structure loose, they simply flung the victims into the open there."

Dr. Blue-Eyes envisioned the people who failed to get away in time, picked up by automated turnstiles and tossed into the open mouth of the volcano.

"...That's a shame. But it was unavoidable. We had no other choice of action."

"Absolutely. Had we done nothing, the people left behind in that place would have died anyway. It was a great success that we were able to save even half of them," Nijo declared. Even though he agreed, the doctor found the way Nijo spoke to be strangely unpleasant.

The younger man closed his laptop. "Well, Doctor, I think I should be on my way soon." He turned his bulging eyes on the aged medical professional.

"Back to Kyoto, you mean?"

"Yes. There's been some family trouble there. I must return at once. You've been a great, great help to me, Doctor. Thanks to you, I've more or less deciphered that code and had a very valuable practical experience in controlling Suikanet. That alone could potentially help me do some amusing things soon."

Nijo yanked the cable out of the wall with tremendous force as he spoke, wound it up, and stuffed it into his case.

Dr. Blue-Eyes was going to reciprocate the statement of gratitude, but he felt that it wouldn't be appropriate to the situation. Nijo's actions had saved the lives of many. However, he was also the reason that the doctor's face was on posters all over Inside, which left the older man feeling it had been more of a hassle than anything.

"I see. Well, let's meet again if anything comes up," he said.

Nijo bowed, then headed to an escalator leading northwest and disappeared.

The statement was never realized. The two never met again.

9

Half a year had passed now.

"Doctor, did you hear? The chunk that got scooped out is filling in again," said Mugino the staffer. Dr. Blue-Eyes was still playing the role of leader at the foot of the mountain.

"Filling in?"

"The part of the mountain that crumbled? There are images on Suikanet. Want to see?"

She turned the screen of her device toward him.

Beneath a blue sky, the clawlike marks where the sector collapse had occurred, leaving behind a jumbled mess of rock and rubble, were now crisscrossed with what looked like gray threads. Although the color was different, it resembled a scab forming on human skin.

"What is all of that?"

"Apparently, it's pipes and girders and things? They've extended over from the adjacent areas, and they're getting thicker. This is what it looked like last month."

Mugino showed him another picture. In this one, there were many people standing atop the roof, observing the hazy scene.

"I see. The structure must be regrowing."

"Regrowing? I've never seen that before. I didn't know Yokohama Station could do that?" replied Mugino. It was the first time Dr. Blue-Eyes had seen it, too, but that was because this was the first time such a large portion of the station had been destroyed.

Dr. Blue-Eyes went to see the regeneration from time to time after that. If he wore the sunglasses he'd asked the station employees to get for him, the brightness wasn't so bad, and because they hid his blue eyes, he could move about in relative peace.

The gray, hazy growth ballooned up in size like a silkworm cocoon. In time, the fibrous materials were no longer visible, becoming more like a bulging white loaf of bread. It seemed to be excreting concrete around the fibers.

After that, the recognizable geometric parts of the station appeared—roofing, stairs, escalators, and glass windows. A year after the eruption, the mountain's appearance had returned to what it was before.

Of course, the structure was simply covering over the earth where the sector collapse happened. The interior wouldn't be the same. It was like packing some stuffing into a tooth cavity. Still, the mountain was so neatly repaired that you couldn't even tell where the collapse had happened.

Many of the families that had evacuated from Hill Town to the foot of the peak started to argue whether or not they should return or remain at the bottom. Some didn't want to go back to the site of such a traumatic experience, while others wanted to, now that they had the chance.

By this time, the chaos in the little city at the foot of the mountain had diminished, and the station employees did not need Dr. Blue-Eyes's reassuring presence to the same degree, so he elected to go back to Hill Town.

After climbing the escalator, he found that his home had been regenerated in the same place it had been previously. It was divided up with bookcases, precisely as it had been before. His massive library was all there, too. Even the rusted metal door to the adjacent room was back.

The only indication that anything had changed was the girl standing there.

"Baa, baa," she said, breaking into a smile when she saw him. Her face was filthy, and trash and sand were caked onto her hair, which reached down to the ground.

He stood and stared at the inexplicable girl until he finally understood.

"Oh...you're alive. How did you get Inside? Did someone give you a Suika?" he asked, placing his hand on her shoulder. The girl just tilted her head and uttered, "Wraah?" It did not seem that she'd learned any more words.

It was the plump little girl the doctor had met on the south side of the mountain, when he'd gone around placing the handicap stones with Nijo. She was somewhat thinner now, however.

"Meh, meh," she said, grinning happily. Her teeth were horrible, and her breath smelled like a dust chute.

◆

Before long, the entire town—in fact, the whole city at the foot of the mountain—knew that Dr. Blue-Eyes was living in the regenerated Hill Town with a girl young enough to be his granddaughter. After the eruption, she had appeared out of nowhere and settled in his home. He named her Kito and began raising her.

Kito grew slowly and learned to call him "Eddie, Eddie," but proved more resistant to learning any other words. She'd probably been abandoned by her parents shortly after birth, then reached the age of six and was expelled by the turnstiles without ever picking up language.

Dr. Blue-Eyes recalled the method of accessing locational data from Nijo and decided to try it out with Kito to see where she'd been.

Yet when he put the device to her hand and executed the command, the response declared that no Suika was detected.

He tried it on his own hand and succeeded at pulling up a map of his life's travels (around the Gunma area and nowhere else).

Mystified, the doctor sought out a bioelectric technician, who pressed his diagnostic tool to Kito's neck in search of a signal. Eventually, his face pale, he gasped. "Dr. Blue-Eyes, what does this mean? She doesn't *have* a Suika."

He gave the technician a quick explanation of Kito's past. He'd found her in a station hollow on the south side of the mountain before the eruption, and left her there initially, but she appeared in the town after it had been regenerated.

The technician considered this, then said, "Meaning that, because the station structure was reconstructed in the eruption, she wound up Inside without a Suika, I guess?"

"Is that possible?"

"No. I've never heard of it," the man answered, worry evident in his expression. Dr. Blue-Eyes impressed upon him in no uncertain terms that he didn't want anyone else to know that the girl did not have a Suika. "Well, if you say so, Doctor," he replied.

Dr. Blue-Eyes wanted to ask Nijo his thoughts, but the net address the man had left behind was no longer working. He'd probably arrived in Kyoto by now. As far as Dr. Blue-Eyes knew, an extremely long distance, individual communication from Gunma to Kyoto was essentially impossible. Perhaps Nijo could pull it off, but there was no communication forthcoming from him.

He was such a loud and obnoxious man when he was here, but he won't get in touch when I really need him.

While the appearance of the books on the shelves was virtually identical to how it was before the eruption, little details had changed about them. Sometimes, the pages were in reverse order, or the same entry repeated hundreds of times, or a section of a literary novel was found smack in the middle of a medical text. The combinations of words and definitions in his dictionary were all scrambled, making it useless. If he'd known this was going to happen, he would have simply given Nijo the dictionary.

10

Mugino rode up the escalator to visit Dr. Blue-Eyes at Hill Town from time to time.

"It's nice to see that things are lively around here again?" she said in that odd way of lifting the ends of her sentences.

"It's only about half as busy as before. Some of the people died, and many more don't want to return. Not that I blame them," he replied, then looked at Kito. "Would you put on some coffee, Kito?"

She answered, "Kii," and began to boil water.

"She's cute. Is that your granddaughter?"

"No. She showed up in town after the eruption. She doesn't seem to have any relatives, so I'm keeping her here," Dr. Blue-Eyes explained. It was the same story he gave the townspeople. Of course, he hadn't told anyone the girl had no Suika.

"Oooh. That's so generous of you, Doctor."

They sat, drinking the coffee Kito made.

"On the south side, all the station staffers are working hard on excavation," Mugino said.

"Excavation?"

"Yep. There wasn't a sector collapse there, but it did turn into a pretty big mess? They're looking around for possible survivors, things that might come in handy, stuff like that."

"On the south side," Dr. Blue-Eyes repeated. As far as he knew, there were still handicap stones around there. Perhaps Nijo still had control of the Suikanet in that region. If only he'd drop a line, in case something happened with Mt. Asama again. "Did they find anything?"

"Not really. There were hardly any people on that side to begin with? Just a bunch of automated turnstile pieces. Oh, but they did recently find something like human bones."

"Bones?"

"That's right. Look."

Mugino showed the doctor her screen.

It was a familiar room—the place where he and Nijo had first met Kito on their trip to set down the handicap stones.

"It's a whole skeleton. Someone must have died there. Probably a child, see?"

Mugino zoomed in on a part of the image. In the gloomy interior, three trash cans stood in a row, and there was a human skeleton atop the couch next to them. Plenty of time had passed since death; almost no flesh remained.

The photo's resolution made it difficult to be sure, but the body appeared roughly a meter in length, like a child around eight or nine years old. Empty plastic wrappers from bakery products littered the area around the bones. A few seemed to have been torn open with teeth.

"...When was this picture taken?"

"Just recently. Um...ah! The nineteenth of last month."

Dr. Blue-Eyes glanced at Kito. A year had passed since she'd showed up in his home following the eruption, and she had grown a little bit, so it was difficult to tell, but he vaguely recalled that she'd been just about the size of those bones when he'd met her in that station hollow.

Did that mean the girl died in that little room?

Then who was the Kito here with him?

After Mugino left, Kito called, "Eddie, Eddie," waving her hands to point out that their stock of coffee was running out.

"Ahh, already out? I'll have to go buy more," muttered Dr. Blue-Eyes.

Kito had learned to do most of the household chores on her own, but she couldn't run errands because she had no Suika. Considering his age, he knew that he'd need to ask someone to look after her in the future. His eyes drifted over his bookcases while he pondered this dilemma.

"There's another one," he muttered. A picture of his wife in a plastic photo frame sat on the shelf.

Dr. Blue-Eyes picked it up, wrote #12 on the frame in pen, then placed it atop a stack of eleven photo frames resting in the corner of the room.

Ever since Hill Town regrew, there had been problems with things multiplying here and there. Some families were heartened by the increase in clothing and food. In Dr. Blue-Eyes's case, for whatever reason, it was the framed picture of his wife.

But the photographs that formed weren't perfect recreations. She had the same clothes and hair, but slight details of her face were different. It was a photograph, supposedly, but there was a whiff of artificiality about it, as though someone had drawn a very detailed picture based on the original image instead. Human eyes were designed to recognize meaning and detail in faces, so even minor changes in angles and curves could make a massive difference in how a person looked.

Sometimes, Dr. Blue-Eyes set up all the photo stands in a row so that he could judge which one looked the most like his wife.

The last time, he felt like the third picture was the closest, but looking at it right now, he felt like the twelfth and newest one was best. But after a moment, he decided that neither one was his wife; the seventh resembled her most accurately. It had the most beautifully composed features. Perhaps that was because he was beautifying her face in his memory.

As he stared at the pictures, each one a slightly different version of his wife's face, Dr. Blue-Eyes grew unsure of what she actually looked like.

Eddie Shimazaki, popularly known as Dr. Blue-Eyes, likely still operates his medical business in Hill Town on the north side of Mt. Asama, accompanied by a girl named Kito, who doesn't have a Suika.

train *(n)*

A connected line of railroad cars. From the verb meaning "to drag behind."

training *(n)*

Instruction, discipline, or drill.

1

July 192 (Station Year), Kumamoto

"I have a question, Instructor."

The young employee raised a hand. The instructor eyed her name tag and saw the tadpole symbol next to the name, indicating a new employee in the training program.

"You have permission to ask, Shimabara," intoned Instructor Yokoi, who wore a short-sleeved uniform. Miika Shimabara lowered her arm ninety degrees, like a clock hand rotating, and pointed out the window.

"Is that a military division training exercise?"

Beyond the glass pane was a bizarre sight. A rope was tied to the rear of a truck, with the other end wrapped around the wrists of a young man who was running behind it. The organic oxide engine belched black smoke as it trundled along slowly but still slightly faster than a human could comfortably run. The young man looked miserable. Moisture from his sweat stained the wheel ruts in the dried earth.

Other new employees were riding on the bed of the truck, along with a few senior employees, who yelled "Run faster!" to the unfortunate man and smacked their hands against the side and back of the truck. Cicadas buzzed and hummed ceaselessly from the woods behind them.

"No," the instructor replied coldly. "That is part of our new member training. All of you are going to undertake the exams soon, and the lowest score of the group will be forced to take the trip back to the dorms in that manner."

An uneasy stir ran through the twenty or so new recruits in the training classroom.

"May I ask one more thing?"

"What?"

"Why would you do that?"

"To ensure you take your training seriously," replied Instructor Yokoi, quite earnestly. "It is our responsibility to maintain the peace of all of Kyushu and protect her lands. As you know, Kyushu has been in conflict with Yokohama Station over the Kanmon Straits for fifty years. So long as the military division, our pride and joy, continues to protect the strait, the fires of war will never come to Kumamoto. But our success demands your focus and dedication at all times."

"Thank you for your answer, sir. I understand now," Miika responded, lowering her head in a manner as smooth and precise as a machine. The instructor asked if anyone else had a question and glanced around the room, but no one raised a hand.

"Then we will conduct a training exercise with weapons today, as planned. Be prepared, because the person who performs the best will be given preferential treatment within the division."

The JR Fukuoka branch in Kumamoto, on the west coast of Kyushu, used buildings that had initially been erected for a different function decades ago. Compared to the headquarters in Hakata and the front-line base in Kitakyushu, the structures were considerably older. They'd originally been made of white concrete, but after so much time, they were all stained black from the soot created by organic oxide reactors.

Located at this base was part of the engineering division, the intelligence division, and the facilities for training new employees.

JR Fukuoka was a government-run business contracted by Japan to oversee the local region during the Winter War. There'd been multiple such entities around the country at the time, but this one always had a stronger military presence due to its geographical proximity to the Korean Peninsula.

However, as the war continued, Yokohama Station's self-replication buried the island of Honshu, and the Japanese government ceased to be about two hundred years ago. With its parent organization lost, this business transformed into a sovereign nation.

With fifty years of successfully holding off the station's creep over the Kanmon Straits under its belt, JR Fukuoka had earned the trust of the Kyushu populace. The police arm of the military division functioned smoothly, public order was tightly maintained, and the worst of their problems was friction between refugees from Shikoku and the native citizens of Kyushu.

The testing range for shooting exams faced a hill on the campus. The mound was very small, only two meters tall, and wooden humanoid targets had been placed at equal intervals along its length. Each one had concentric circles where the heart would be on a living person.

Instructor Yokoi held up an electric pump gun to demonstrate what the trainees would be using. It was a weapon developed in the Winter War that could use any piece of metal as a bullet. With the ability to find ammo anywhere, soldiers could fight for months without needing to resupply. According to what they taught in history class, this turned all of the military arenas of the world into chaotic guerilla battles that allowed the conflict to persist until it had entirely burned out any remaining shreds of civilization.

Guns were standard among Kyushu civilians for self-defense, but only short ones with twenty-centimeter barrels were legal, and they didn't do much more than slow down an enemy. The weapons used in firing training here were JR Fukuoka's own eighty-centimeter-long guns; they had a monopoly on the production and possession of them. The armament was about as thick as Miika's arm, but it wasn't that heavy when slung over the shoulder because most of the interior was hollow space for the projectile's acceleration.

Even when Instructor Yokoi wasn't speaking, his mouth was open. He probably had a bad nose and could only breathe through his mouth. Due to the dryness this caused, he always carried around a water bottle with him.

"We'll be using these pellets. They have the least trajectory curvature," he stated, holding up a metal ball about a centimeter across. "However, you don't know what you might be using in a battle. You can learn how to shoot with ideal bullets like these, but success comes down to instinct. If you don't understand after watching, you're not going to after a lesson, either."

In other words, it was an aptitude test to see if the new employees had the smarts to fire a weapon they'd learned nothing about, Miika surmised. She didn't quite know what to expect from actual combat, though.

"I have a question."

"Yes?"

"What is the purpose of practicing with these guns?" Miika inquired.

The instructor glared at her mockingly. "To protect the population."

"Who are we supposed to shoot to protect the population?"

"Being able to judge that on your own is what separates fully-fledged adults from the rest."

"I understand, sir."

When her turn came around, Miika loaded six of the metal balls into the gun she was given, as instructed. The bullets seemed unnaturally small for the size of the weapon.

It was her first time handling a long gun, but the item's construction was straightforward and easy to use. The metal pellets had just a faint scent of earth to them. Undoubtedly, they'd been used in training exercises like this one before. Collecting them from the dirt had to be a chore.

After ensuring that the firing mode was set to single shot, she pulled the trigger.

Pam! Boosh. A small hole was gouged out of the flank of the human target. Miika lowered the barrel and shot twice more. Each one hit a knee.

"Are you aware that you get a higher score for hitting the heart?" questioned a senior employee holding the scoring chart behind her.

"I determined that aiming for the legs would be a better means of controlling the enemy's range of motion."

"Look, this is a test, so just do as the instructions say."

Miika exhaled with undisguised frustration. "Yes, sir."

She raised the barrel and fired. The pellet grazed the target's shoulder and bounced off the dirt behind it. Then she lowered slightly and fired the two remaining bullets into the chest.

"See? You *can* do it," the man said. He wrote *Military Division Aptitude: B* on the scoring sheet. The grades went from A to E.

Mika thought it was much easier to adjust your aim during the exam if you hit the target on the first try and more difficult if you didn't. In fact, the new hire who took the test after her missed by a wide margin, striking the dirt behind the target. The next shot hit the ground, and that left the pupil totally rattled. His hands shook as he continued, and each of the last four rounds missed the mark.

Instructor Yokoi told him, "You should try your luck with the intelligence division."

Everyone understood the derision behind that statement. The unlucky young man ended up dragged behind that truck at the end of the day.

Although it was not recorded in any official capacity, everyone knew there was a clear hierarchy among the various sections of JR Fukuoka. The military division was on top, and next came engineering. Given that the company's entire purpose was to protect the homeland and its people from Yokohama Station across the strait, that priority would never change. Next came several administrative-type divisions, and last was the intelligence division.

Those who fought at the strait were the most important, and the engineers who made their weapons were the second most crucial. Their purposes were the easiest to understand. The intelligence division was the lowest rung because nobody really knew what they were good for.

2

"Miika Shimabara, your marks are good enough for you to go to JR. I will write you a letter of recommendation," her schoolteacher had told her a year ago.

"I'm honored," she had replied. The teacher was very kind and helpful, the sort of person who said, "If there's anything you don't understand, just ask the question."

At this point, Miika could no longer remember why she had said it was an honor. All she could recall was that it was considered a respectable career path among the students at the school.

Historically speaking, educational length corresponded to social worth. In the High Civilization era, there were students at age twenty-five and even thirty. But in present-day Kyushu, those who stayed in school until twenty were the elites, and only a small portion of them served in the governing company known as JR Fukuoka.

In other words, the people here had finished their education at the same time they became legal adults.

The door had only the room number and the name of the one in charge written on it. She knocked twice and, once she heard a response from within, quietly pushed it open.

"It's nice to meet you. My name is Miika Shimabara, and I was placed in this division today," she stated mechanically, bowing in the doorway. Men sitting at desks pointed toward the wall turned in her direction one at a time, then looked at each other in confusion. Their faces said that they weren't supposed to get anyone like *her*.

For a moment, she started to worry she'd knocked on the wrong door. Then a middle-aged man wearing a white coat appeared from the back. "Ah, Miss Shimabara. Welcome."

He was Sugimoto, the leader of the chemistry team of JR Fukuoka's engineering division. The others quickly returned to their work.

"Boy, it sure heated up quick today, didn't it? Aren't you hot dressed like that, Miss Shimabara?" asked Sugimoto, fanning himself with a hard file folder while staring at her up and down. Underneath the coat, he seemed to be wearing only a T-shirt.

"It said this was our summer uniform," Miika replied. All of the company buildings had internal cooling, so she was cold, if anything. It seemed like a waste when there wasn't enough energy to regulate the civilian homes, but given that most of the employees were men, there might not be any point in arguing.

"Well, we aren't as strict on the rules as the military, so relax, and we'll all get along fine. As for your seat and such, well…"

Sugimoto had an odd way of pausing as he talked. He walked toward the back of the large room, and Miika followed. There was a complex, chaotic scent typical to rooms that held a large number of people. It was two o'clock, and it smelled as though some people had just been eating lunch. *This seat had mustard, and this one soy sauce,* Miika guessed, and then she caught a whiff of perfume. It was the kind of odor she wouldn't have expected to encounter in a place like this.

"Can you show her around, Miss Kuroki?" Sugimoto called out to the opposite wall.

"Oh! Yes!" replied a pleased female voice from behind a partition. The owner emerged—a woman whose beauty startled Miika.

The rainy season was over, and summer had arrived in earnest. After their three-month training period, the new employees were shipped off to their respective assignments in smoke-belching trucks. However, because Miika had been assigned to the engineering division's chemistry team, she remained at the Kumamoto branch.

In the Hakata main office, they performed lots of practical work like developing weapons, but the officers in Kumamoto mainly were dedicated to deciphering pre-war texts and recreating their technology. Much of humanity's accumulated knowledge had been scattered during the Winter War, and this office's task was to scrounge up what reference materials survived, to see if they proved useful. There was a common saying around the office: "In Kumamoto, you learn more about ancient kanji than chemical formulas."

The primary success of the chemistry team was the development of the fibrous material known as structural genetic field-resistant polymer. It was highly effective at blocking the contamination of the structural genetic field attached to the material that Yokohama Station flung over the Kanmon Straits from Honshu. Naturally, this earned very high praise from JR Fukuoka headquarters, whose top priority above all was keeping the station from taking hold on Kyushu.

"It utilizes a conductive polymer, you see," Kuroki explained while showing Miika some company materials. "It's difficult to acquire a sample contaminated by the structural genetic field, but we got a hint from the way the station can't cross the ocean. Do you know what that means?"

"Yes. Like seawater, the conductivity disperses the structural genetic field, but unlike metal, it has no free electrons, which means it can't be infected by the structural genetic field itself," Miika recited according to what she'd studied ahead of time.

Kuroki looked amazed. "You're good, Mii."

"So what is the team working on now?"

"Our group is working on recycling waste liquid from heavy metals."

"Waste liquid?"

"It comes out of here," Kuroki replied, pointing at the map. To the east of the Kanmon Straits, past a stretch of water called Suo-nada, a cape jutted south from Honshu. "There are many points where Yokohama Station dumps into the water, but the material is different depending on the location. Around here, there are lots of rare metals."

"You can acquire mineral resources from the station?"

"Yes. But it's a bit of a slurry of various elements, so we're researching how we might separate them effectively. Some of the waste is composed of rare materials you can't get anymore, so this is a very important job."

Miika nodded vigorously at the phrase *important job*. "When you say separate them, you mean through electrolysis, adding electrons to ionized metal to reduce them."

"Yes!" said Kuroki. She was delighted every time Miika correctly described something. "It's nothing but men on this team, so I've been really excited all week after I heard we'd get a girl this year. I'm so happy."

The entire company was about 85 percent men, but the engineering division was where that ratio was pushed the furthest. Miika knew through experience that when a woman joined a team of mostly men, it was the minority of women who were actually more excited about it than the men.

"I'll do my best to grow and meet your expectations. It's a pleasure to be here."

"Expectations?" Kuroki repeated. She chuckled. "Mii, you ought to relax a little and be more casual about things."

"What do you mean?"

"If you keep coming into the office like you did today, people are going to freak out and think it's a surprise inspection from the conduct division. There are investigations fairly often within the company, although not so often in our office."

"I apologize. I will be careful about that."

"Listen, Mii, you don't have to talk like you're at a job interview. Relax a little."

"I understand."

The issue was that this was just how Miika talked. She knew it was weird, but it was the style she'd adopted, and there was no changing it now.

They told her to show up at nine in the morning and leave at five in the afternoon, so Miika decided to arrive at eight thirty and leave at five thirty. In the morning, she worked on deciphering and sorting documents, and in the afternoon, she learned how to use the tools in the lab. JR's laboratory was very impressive and much more advanced than the one she'd studied in at school.

"I have a question, sir," she said to Foreman Sugimoto when he handed her some forms.

"What is it, Miss Shimabara?"

"I noticed that your lab coat does not smell like chemicals at all."

The only odor clinging to his clothes was the one belonging to all men his age. He cleaned his attire often, though, so most people probably wouldn't even notice it. Miika didn't think it smelled bad.

"My actual lab coat I wear during experiments is in my locker. The ladies in the mess hall don't like it when I wear it in there. I keep it separate from my ordinary wear, you see." Sugimoto chuckled. Miika couldn't tell if he was joking or serious, but she replied, "I understand," anyway.

"You've got a very sharp nose, Miss Shimabara."

"I've heard that before."

"That might make the chemistry team unpleasant for you. We work with plenty of things that smell downright awful. So…good luck."

"I'm fine. In fact, I don't have any problems with chemical odors," Miika responded quickly. She did not want them to identify her as having poor aptitude for her new assignment. While her nose was quite discerning when it came to picking out particular scents, her advanced sensitivity didn't mean she was grossed out by more smells than the average person—with a few exceptions.

"Is there anything about the job that's causing you trouble so far?"

"No. Everything is going well. Miss Kuroki gives excellent guidance. If anything seems off, it's that I've noticed many people not abiding by the start and end of work hours," she said.

The team leader considered this. "Well, our job doesn't exactly require us to be punctual, to be fair. It would be a different story if we were in the military division."

"I understand. But if we do not mind our time precisely, it will make us less efficient as an organization…"

"You have a point. If you're here early and Kuroki is late, that leaves you with no one to instruct you," he said.

Miika felt like he was taking her comment as a criticism of Kuroki and hastily added, "No, sir. I'm sure it's harder for people with families to make the proper time, after all."

"Huh?" the team leader asked, taken aback.

"Isn't Miss Kuroki married?"

"Huh? I've never heard as much. And I've known her since she joined the company."

"But she's pregnant."

"She is?" His eyes were wide. Miika suddenly regretted her comments. It was a very subtle thing, not something the average person would notice. "Did she tell you that?" he continued.

"…No, sir. Perhaps I was mistaken. I'm very sorry for my comment," she said, shaking her head. It was such a different gesture from Miika's usual clockwork precision that the man gave the young woman a suspicious look.

When he returned to his office, Miika examined the materials he'd given her, regretting her lack of discretion. Every time she committed one of these mistakes, she worked harder to comport herself properly. It had been a habit of hers ever since she was a child.

Miika's observance of the schedule was so precise, in fact, that people started to claim she was an android developed by the mechanics division. She was used to that. It made things easier for her if people treated her like a machine. Being treated like too much of a human being had the potential to throw off her rhythm.

And so it was two months after her assignment that Miika had to deal with something that threw off her rhythm like nothing she'd ever experienced before.

3

"Huh? Ah yes. Of course. I understand. The dormitory. I see. I'll be right over there."

She could hear Foreman Sugimoto's voice coming through the

open doorway of his little office. There was still a bit of time before the workday started, so only a few others besides Miika were in the building.

Sugimoto emerged from the office and said, "Er, good morning, everyone." He looked around the large open office of the chemistry team. "Is there anyone with nothing else to do who might come and help me? Yoshida, and…ah, Miss Shimabara, you come, too."

"Yes, sir." Miika put down the files she was about to read at her desk.

"There's been a bit of a happening in the company. They need us to take a look at it, so you'll have to do."

Miika found herself heading toward the worker dormitory with Yoshida, an older employee with tanned skin. The dormitory was where new hires lived during their training period and where employees could sleep during long, intensive work sessions. Unmarried employees could also request to live there semi-permanently.

September in Kumamoto was still muggy and sticky. After the rain the night before, the odor of geosmin wafted up from below. The three of them trod on soggy ground as they made their way to the dormitory, where an odd scent became apparent to Miika.

"Did a wild bear wander into the building?" she asked.

"Why do you ask that?"

"I smell blood. Did they kill it already?"

Behind her, Yoshida muttered that the bears on Kumamoto had already gone extinct.

"Hmm. Well, you're not far off, I suppose. Here, put these on," Sugimoto said, handing gloves and masks to the two. He stepped up to a door and checked the room number. "Just don't be too shocked when you see inside."

After he'd pulled the knob, the smell of blood got much stronger. A young man from the military division stood at the window and greeted Sugimoto politely when they walked in. Then he noticed Miika and Yoshida and gave them a suspicious, worried look. According to his employee badge, he was in the conduct division, the part of the military that focused on eliminating corruption.

There was a person lying faceup on the bed. His face was red, as though splattered by tomatoes. But on closer inspection, it was not smeared with a red substance but had instead been gouged out. The throat was blown wide open, the jaw had fallen off, and the facial muscles were visible. Almost none of the teeth were left.

The man's large figure and hairy arms sticking out of his short-sleeved shirt were familiar. Behind Miika, Yoshida made a guttural convulsion.

"This is…Instructor Yokoi, isn't it?"

"You know him, Miss Shimabara?" asked Sugimoto calmly.

"Yes. He was in charge of my onboarding training period."

"I see. So he's doing instruction now, eh?"

The man from the conduct division said, "The time of death was about two in the morning, apparently. He didn't show up for work, so someone came to check if he was in his room and discovered he'd lost his face."

"So it's a homicide, then. Was his room locked?" Yoshida inquired.

The conduct member looked at the clipboard in his hand. "The door was not locked, it says." Yoshida appeared disappointed for some reason.

"Foreman," Miika called softly.

"You have a question?"

"Yes. Is handling this incident part of the chemistry team's job? Not the conduct division?"

"Good question. I can't recall many things like this happening. But circumstances being what they are…," Sugimoto said, sounding troubled.

"Do murders happen often within the company?"

"It's been a long time since a body turned up. When was the last one?"

"Ten years ago," answered the conduct member.

"Ah yes. But that wasn't murder so much as a riot, wasn't it? Some extremists connected to the refugees from Shikoku made their way into a company building. The poor girl at the company store fell victim. At the time, we marshaled all the civilians, looked at fingerprints, and got all the evidence we needed."

Miika had seen that on the news. The head of the military division at the time had lambasted the horrid actions of the attackers and delivered an impassioned speech at the victim's funeral. She remembered the words being very frightening to her as a child. After a thorough investigation, the extremists were wiped out.

"But it's not going to be easy to clean it up that way. This is very likely an inside job."

"Why is that?"

"The dormitory is automatically locked at eight o'clock. You need an employee badge to go in or out after that," explained the conduct division man.

"Ah, that makes sense. So for it to be an outsider, they would have had to hide in this building for at least six hours, until two in the morning, when the crime happened. That would be difficult," said Yoshida.

Miika looked at what remained of Instructor Yokoi's face. During Miika's shooting instruction, he'd told her to be the judge of whom to shoot to protect the populace. If the person who did this was a company member, they had judged the necessity of the matter and decided to shoot the instructor.

"Perhaps it was a small grenade," Yoshida offered.

Sugimoto chuckled at that. "A classic trope. Yoshida, do you like old war movies? If it was an explosion like that, there would be metal shrapnel and damage all over the place."

"Then maybe they filled the room with flammable gas. And when the victim tried to smoke a cigarette and sparked a light, boom."

"That would have blown out the windows. And you'd have to completely surround him with gas. In purely entropic terms, it's hard to accomplish."

"And he doesn't smoke," added Miika.

"Is that right, Miss Shimabara?"

"Yes. If he had smoked within the past three months, I would know by the smell. Also, I don't think explosives of any kind were utilized. Assuming we're talking about the same kind used close to the station."

"Very impressive," marveled Sugimoto. For some reason, Yoshida looked just a little irritated. The team leader asked, "Was there anything here that could have been the weapon?"

The conduct member produced a short gun in a clear plastic bag. "Only thing left in the room was this electric pump gun. This was the victim's personal firearm."

"Hmm. You couldn't kill a person with this. It'd probably hurt like hell if you used a sharp piece of metal as a bullet, but it certainly wouldn't blow someone's face off," Sugimoto remarked.

"Perhaps they gouged his face off with a knife."

"You've got a very grotesque imagination, Miss Shimabara. Do you like gory movies? Anyway, it'd be tough to cut someone up while they were sleeping. They'd wake up," he replied with a laugh. Miika had noticed that Sugimoto would chuckle about almost anything.

Judging by the map of the building, this room was all the way in the corner of the dormitory. Next door was a large group space used during the new recruit training period, but no one was there at this time of year. A bit of noise late at night wasn't going to attract any attention here.

Nearly a hundred employees had stayed at the dormitory last night, but almost no one was out walking the halls in the middle of the night.

"In other words, it could have been anyone," stated the conduct member.

"Pretty tough situation," Sugimoto observed with a laugh. "We can do a weapon search as a matter of protocol. I'm guessing it might be a better idea to look into the building entry history."

"Yes, we are working on that, too."

"Entry history?" interrupted Miika.

Yoshida explained, "The building is automatically locked at eight o'clock at night. You need an employee ID to get in or out after that. So there should be a record of everyone who came in."

"That would be this," said the man from the conduct division, showing them a flat device. It contained a list of all the people who had opened the locked door between eight last night to this morning and the times at which they did so. There were a few dozen entries.

"This list doesn't make sense," Yoshida commented. "Foreman, part of this entry history has been deleted."

"What? How can you tell?"

"About ten o'clock last night, I passed by the dormitory to buy a can of coffee from the vending machine outside, and I just happened to see someone I know entering the building. There's no mention of that here," he replied proudly.

This caught Sugimoto's interest. "Who was it?"

"A man named Okuma from the intelligence division."

"Ah, I see. So you're suggesting he sneaked in here, then deleted his instance from the building's entry history."

"The intelligence division is who controls the entry history to begin with, so that's quite possible."

"Hmm." Sugimoto considered this. "Miss Shimabara, I hate to ask, but could you go to the intelligence division and call Okuma here to speak with us?"

"Me?" Miika said. She glanced at the conduct division man next to her.

"If a military man goes, he might figure out what's going on and cover up any evidence. But there's much less danger of that if he's approached by, er, a young woman like you."

"Doesn't Mr. Yoshida know him already?"

"If I go, it's only going to get messy. Please, Shimabara, you gotta do this for us," Yoshida pleaded.

Here we go again, she thought. When she was the only woman in a group of men, she knew from experience that they tended to push the most menial tasks onto her.

"Miss Kuroki said that I have the demeanor of a soldier," she asserted.

Sugimoto and Yoshida looked at each other, then tilted their heads and raised their eyebrows as if to say, *Yes, that seems right.*

4

The intelligence division building was small and old in comparison to the others. It was in a corner near the rear gate that was so rusted it hardly ever moved. The structure and its location seemed a very accurate representation of the division's esteem within the company.

Right past the entrance was a door reading INTELLIGENCE 3RD DIVISION. Next to it was a magnetic plate for managing attendance, with all the member names written next to columns for PRESENT, ON CAMPUS, and AT HOME, but the magnets to mark each column were nowhere to be seen.

On the list of names was an Okuma with an ambiguous kanji for his given name. Miika knocked on the door, but there was no response.

It was clear that no lights were on inside through the frosted glass. It was ten in the morning. Perhaps they were having a meeting somewhere.

Just then, the adjacent door opened, and a man with exceedingly narrow eyes emerged. The entire left side of his hair was sticking up, like the world's worst cowlick, and he was scratching his head.

Miika bowed and said, "Pardon me. I'm Shimabara, with the engineering division's chemistry team. I have a question."

The sleepy-eyed man twitched, his shoulders jumping, and he said, "Yes, what is it?!" in a surprisingly high-pitched voice. His eyes opened wide enough that she could make out some of his pupils.

"Where might I find the 'Hayahiko' Okuma from this office?"

"Uh, if you want Okuma, I don't think he's shown up yet. It's still before noon," he answered, then turned back and yelled through the doorway. "Hey, has anyone seen Okuma today?"

"Nooo. If he's anywhere, it'd be the smoking room, don't you think?" replied a voice. The mention of a smoking room made Miika grimace.

"There you have it. I'd try the smoking room if I were you."

She followed the sleepyhead's suggestion and headed for the smoking room at the corner of the hall. It was a cramped little chamber with a large vent fan in the middle and frosted glass walls facing the hallway. The partially opaque pane was likely not intentional but the result of built-up grime from years upon years of smoke. Two silhouettes were standing within, one fat and one thin, their backs to the hall. The room was clearly not soundproofed, because their conversation was audible.

"Based on images we've excavated from the input layer, that black bear icon shows up in all public facilities, such as rail stations and airports. It's clear that the bear was worshipped as a kind of god in the region," the thin person said, speaking rapidly.

"Classic example of animism," replied the fat person. "But why are the bear's pupils so tiny? They look like a cat's."

"I think the design incorporates the details of other animals. This is something you see in myths quite a lot. It's my theory that the name Kumamoto might even refer to this god."

"Hey, there's someone behind us."

The two turned around to look at Miika through the smoky glass. From what she could see, they were only holding cigarettes. In this circumstance, at least, she didn't need to worry about them destroying evidence.

"Is Hayahiko Okuma of the intelligence division present? I've heard that he frequents this spot," Miika explained.

The two men shared a look.

"Did you screw something up?"

"I dunno. But I've certainly done my share of things."

"Just not your job."

"Why, yes I do."

"People know to look for you in the smoking room, though."

The men seemed perfectly content to bicker among themselves rather than reply to her. In the back, there was a whiteboard, upon which was a number of messages Miika could make out.

Okuma +13 Sakuma -11 Togo +17 Li -19

Leave Work On Time Month in effect (does not guarantee actually leaving on time)

I've completely deciphered Codama language.

The station structure can take root on Nokonoshima?

The thinner of the two men, Okuma, cleared his throat and announced through the glass wall, "Thank you for coming. Did you want something from me?"

"You're Mr. Okuma from the intelligence division?"

"Yes. That is exactly who I am."

"My name is Shimabara, and I'm from the engineering division chemistry team. You've been summoned. Please come with me," Miika requested. They told her to bring him without putting him on guard, and he did not seem to be concerned in the least. If anything, he seemed to be mocking her.

"Chemistry team…? Ah, all right. Just let me finish this butt."

"It's an urgent call."

"What, did you open an e-mail virus?"

"The conduct division is waiting. Please don't waste our salaried time, sir."

"If they're using an employee to call over another employee, they shouldn't be complaining about the cost. An e-mail would do perfectly fine," Okuma grumbled, pressing his half-smoked cigarette into the ashtray installed on the table before he opened the door.

As it swung open, Miika stepped three meters back. Okuma watched her with undisguised skepticism.

She was used to having an extremely adept sense of smell, and she could withstand almost anything—with a few exceptions.

5

"I didn't know they had these for the employees in the holding area," Okuma said before laughing from behind the bars.

The young man from the conduct division proudly read off the document calling for Okuma's apprehension, and they smoothly took him to the holding area on campus. After they described the state of Instructor Yokoi's murder, his smoking-room loquaciousness evaporated entirely, and he maintained total silence on the trip.

When he was left in the holding area with only Miika for company, he finally began to talk again while seated on the tatami.

"This is quite comfortable. The bedding's clean enough, and I don't have to work. If there's any problem, it's that I can't smoke here."

"Ah, I see," Miika replied.

Miika had seen the cells for regular civilians. They were structured the same way as the employee cells, but each contained more people and was much busier. Nearly all of the imprisoned citizens were those who'd committed theft out of desperation, so there was a perpetual whiff of misery in there. Compared to that environment, Okuma's room had seen much less use and was cleaner.

"I figured I'd get imprisoned sooner or later for slacking off at work. I didn't expect it'd be on suspicion of murder. I've been working here for four years, but that's one I didn't see coming."

"You didn't see it coming? You weren't arguing your case, so I assumed you were giving up and admitting your guilt."

"Well, I don't want to say anything that the conduct division might use against me. And I have no idea why I'm a suspect in the first place."

"Because we have information that you improperly deleted your record of entering the dormitory."

"Huh?"

"So you didn't delete the record?"

"That's weird. There shouldn't have been any record of the log being edited," Okuma said suspiciously. "And I'm the manager of that database, so I should know."

"That doesn't matter. What matters is why you were erasing your tracks," Miika replied accusingly.

Okuma went quiet for a bit, then clapped his hands. "Oh! There was a witness. That's where I screwed up. That's my fault. Well, damn. It's true that I tweaked the entry history, but I didn't kill that guy. I can tell you that much."

"Then what did you do?" Miika pressed. She already had a guess, however. The dormitory was a five-story building, and the top floor was reserved for women.

"I was meeting with Mr. Togo."

"Togo?"

"The round fella I was with in the smoking room. He's a coworker in the intelligence division. He lives in the dorm."

"What were you doing?"

"Playing poker."

"Poker?"

"It's a card game. You try to make the best hand possible out of five cards."

"I know what poker is. Why did you need to delete your entry history for that? Leisure time outside of work hours isn't prohibited. As long as you weren't gambling."

"Oh, you're a goodie two-shoes, huh?" Okuma chuckled. "Anyway, you can ask Mr. Togo, and he'll tell you. I was playing poker in his room from ten to midnight."

"The estimated time of the murder was around two o'clock."

"I went back after midnight. That's the thing about us knowledge specialists: We have to sleep at a good hour."

"Do you have a record of when you left?"

"Uh…there's a backup, yes, but the fact that I'm the one who manages it doesn't make it admissible evidence, does it?" Okuma said. "By that logic, though, everyone living in the dormitory and everyone else who entered or left is a suspect, too. There are a hundred possible killers. Why am I the only one in here?"

"Obviously, it's because you were illicitly erasing the building's entry history."

"Well, you got me there," he admitted, and he bit his nails. Okuma seemed to be unable to relax without something in his mouth. It was a common phenomenon among heavy smokers.

"Okay, I understand why I'm in here. But why are you, uh, Shimabara? You're with the chemistry team."

"I'm not entirely sure, either. For some reason, the chemistry team is conducting an investigation of the murder."

"Ah. So our distribution of duties is breaking down. That's a common feature in companies experiencing institutional fatigue," Okuma remarked, as though it wasn't his problem.

"Yes, the kind of company where a member of the intelligence division deletes information improperly," Miika shot back.

Evidently delighted at the way she talked back to him, Okuma stated, "Let me be clear. Our job isn't to falsify company data or ponder the root of the name Kumamoto in our smoking room."

It was an excuse without a shred of believability, she thought. "What sort of work do you do, then?"

"Data excavation on the JR Integrated Intelligence."

"...?"

"It's an artificial intelligence that used all of Japan's networks back during the war. They say that was the start of Yokohama Station's expansion. But because of the station, it's not functioning anymore."

"I already know that." It was something Miika had learned during history lessons at school.

"We're extracting information from the station units left in Kyushu to see what we might be able to use."

"That actually sounds like a very worthwhile job," said Miika, surprised. That would mean the materials Foreman Sugimoto gave her to read from before the war had been recovered by the intelligence division.

"Don't treat me like an idiot. I *do* do my job."

"Yet you admitted that you slack off at work."

"Well, I don't. I am actively engaged in making it more logically sound."

Internally, Miika grappled with the idea that adults like Okuma actually existed. She cleared her throat. "So if there's leftover data from the JR Integrated Intelligence, then is it possible you might find a way of counteracting the station?"

"If only," Okuma answered with a sigh. "There are multiple layers to the information. Basically, the things humans taught the intelligence and things it thought based on those teachings. The former is just digital data, so all we need to do is convert it to a modern format. But the latter is impossible to figure out. Even though it has a physical structure, it does not take any form that is intelligible to a human being."

Miika used her imagination to grapple with the concept. "So it's like the brain is stored in formaldehyde all on its own?"

"That's a good way of putting it," replied Okuma, impressed. "But in this case, it's an alien's brain."

"All right, sir. I do understand that you perform your job. So if you've got anything to say regarding this crime, now's the time to come forward. You can insist on your innocence, if you desire. I don't wish to be involved in this incident, either."

"What am I supposed to say?" Okuma chewed on his nails some more. "Hmm. Could you tell me more about the crime scene? Bring me reference materials on it. If the chemistry team is in charge of the investigation, you should have access to that."

"Why should I?"

"You said you didn't want to do this, right? We'll solve it faster if I can see the materials."

"Why would I aid a potential murderer?"

"Who cares? It's not going to hurt anything. C'mon, show a little trust in me."

"Why should I trust you?" Miika questioned, glaring. "Did you really not kill the instructor?"

"Of course I didn't. You think I'd do something so awful?"

"I do not know your character well enough to judge. I know you're in the intelligence division, you gamble in violation of company rules, and you smoke a pack a day. That's it," Miika stated. Being able to tell how much a person smoked by their smell was one of her less pleasant abilities. She only mentioned it as a warning that he should cut back, but she didn't know if he was the kind of man who was perceptive enough to take the hint.

"Uh-huh. So you know nothing about me," Okuma decided, apparently satisfied. "Okay. Let's extrapolate from there. If you were walking down the street and saw an unfamiliar man smoking a cigarette, would you think, 'That man would probably commit murder'?"

"No."

"Then you should believe in my innocence."

"Your logic is awful."

"Why don't you understand?" Okuma asked, exasperated.

Miika was feeling frustrated, too; she just didn't let it show.

"All right, fine. I'll tell you what I know," Okuma said, rocking backward and forward on the dirty tatami mats. "First of all, the conduct division definitely wants to handle this internally, if possible. In other words, they don't want the populace to know there's been a murder within the company. They can't hide that there was a death, I assume, so they'd like to have it reported in the news as accidental. But they have to find the killer first."

"Why do you say that?"

"Because they're saddling you with the investigation. If it was a normal incident, they could easily go outside to solve it."

"To a civilian source, you mean."

"Plus, we've got a victim whose face was carved off—a very brutal way to kill. There are a few reasons someone might choose such a cruel and disfiguring method."

"Political reasons. The possibility that this was a terrorist incident."

"That's one of them. There are plenty of anti-JR sentiments on the island. But that's unlikely in this case. A terrorist would choose a more public place to strike than at a company dorm late at night. And there's been no statement trumpeting their involvement."

"Perhaps it was a sadistic murder. Someone who derived pleasure from cutting off the face of another," Miika suggested.

Okuma didn't reply right away. "I...didn't think of that. Perhaps. And then, although orthodox, you have the possibility of a personal grudge. Someone who'd suffered under that man to the point that it pushed them to murder him in the most gruesome method conceivable. If that's the case, then we're in trouble. There are so many potential subjects, we'll never narrow them down."

"The instructor was a very strict and tough man, but I don't know if he would inspire that kind of hatred."

"Huh?" Okuma gaped, staring at Miika with incredulity. It seemed he was mocking her. "Listen, that guy was a real asshole, just a major piece of shit. Everyone learned that quick during training."

"Is that right?"

"He was in personnel, you see. The guy would abuse his privileges like crazy."

"Aren't you in that cell right now because you were abusing your privileges?"

"Yeah, but I earned this. Don't lump me in with someone who

actually made others' lives hell," Okuma argued proudly. "Anyway, part of the issue is that the personnel division exists at all. Why do we need an entire group just for managing people? If some are talented and others are useless, that should be up to those who actually work with them to decide. It makes no sense that an independent department just *decides* these things from on high. Being in that position of judgment rots a person from the inside out. You turn out like him."

Momentum built up as Okuma spoke so that the last few sentences tumbled out in a rush. Miika vaguely recalled how the whiteboard in the smoking room had things like *Okuma +13* and *Sakuma –11* written on it.

"What happened with him?"

"I don't want to go into detail. He crossed the line between public and private. All you need to see is the sadistic way he conducted his training programs. If anyone complained about it, he would shuffle them off to other regions. He was a womanizer, too."

"Have you ever fired a gun, Mr. Okuma?"

"...Why would you ask that?"

"I was just wondering."

"I fired one during training," Okuma answered. "They gave me an E aptitude for the military division. Haven't shot one since then."

"I see."

That probably meant he had been dragged behind that smoke-belching truck. Okuma could likely sense from Miika's reaction that she was envisioning that picture, and it made him scowl.

"For one thing," he said, "the idea that you can accurately fire a gun is ridiculous. There's over a meter of distance between your brain and your fingertips. The only people who can move objects over a meter away with absolute precision are psychics or freaks."

"So you only consider your brain to be 'yourself'?"

"Of course. Otherwise, who would bother to create prosthetic limbs?"

Miika felt like she was starting to understand what made this man tick, although she'd never wished to be privy to that knowledge.

6

"I don't see what's wrong with showing him the materials. As he says, he can't cover up anything from the holding cell, and the more minds working on this, the better. I'd like to get this cleared up as soon as possible, too. I'll go and tell the fellow from the conduct division," Sugimoto had stated casually.

Thus, Miika found herself carrying a stack of printouts to Okuma. It infuriated her to do as the unlikable smoker had asked, but she couldn't protest in Sugimoto's presence. She headed for the holding cell in a huff, upset that she wasn't able to get back to her job.

"The only thing present at the scene that would serve as a weapon was a short-barreled electric pump gun. The only prints on it belonged to the victim. This was the old man's personal gun, huh?" Okuma commented while eyeing the sheets of paper.

"So it seems," Miika responded. It wasn't rare for company employees to carry armaments. The short guns worked the same way as the long ones employed to maintain public order. They all expelled an accelerated piece of metal from the end—but the shorter guns were far weaker. They were like slightly more powerful slingshots. The force was enough to slow a target, but that was it.

"So his face explodes, and he dies. There's a high possibility that explosives were used, but there are no traces of gunpowder or smoke. Instead, inside his mouth is... What is that? Cloth?"

"It's charred cotton. Not any kind of guncotton."

"That figures. If they had shoved guncotton in his mouth, it would still need to be ignited somehow," Okuma said, flipping through the stapled stack of paper.

"About the conversation from yesterday..."

"Yeah?"

"If I saw an unfamiliar man smoking on the street, and there was a dead body at his feet, I would think he'd probably killed that person. In other words, the analogy you used yesterday ignores the fact that there must be a dead body present."

"Listen, outside the station, a split-second decision can have life-and-death consequences. A military woman shouldn't be debating the logic of an argument she had the day before."

"This is not a battlefield. We're behind the front line, where careful, cautious decision-making is required. Also, I'm on the chemistry team of the engineering division," Miika asserted, showing him her ID through the bars.

"Oh, right. You're with the chemistry team. Anyway, there was a short gun at the scene, huh?"

Okuma looked up at the ceiling and bit his nails. It was more voracious than usual, a rapid, audible clicking. After ten seconds of this, he said, "So...did you do it, then?" and looked at Miika.

Without batting an eye, she replied, "I did not."

"Then it was someone else on the chemistry team."

Miika's eyes widened subtly. "Why do you say that?"

"I mean, it just makes sense. Don't you get it?"

"I don't get it. You are insulting my team."

"I'm not. It's the logical conclusion."

"Very well. You should be grateful that these metal bars exist between you and my fist, sir," Miika stated, clenching her hand.

Okuma snorted with laughter. "You can bet on it. The killer is someone on the chemistry team. And if I'm wrong..."

"You must stop smoking," she answered at once.

"Sure thing, but what do you gain out of that?"

"One less smoker in the world is all the profit I need."

"Well, listen to you. Then if I win, you have to buy me a whole carton from the store near the front entrance. I'll even give you the money for it."

"Interesting. So you would find entertainment in the act of sending me to buy cigarettes, knowing that I despise them."

"I can see why you're in engineering. You're smarter than a soldier," acknowledged Okuma. "Anyway, do this task for me. Pick out everyone from the chemistry team who went in or out of the dorm that night."

"You're the one who manages that data, correct?"

"Yet to my shock, I am not currently in possession of my computer,"

Okuma responded, spreading his hands to show they were empty. "If you ask that conduct division guy, I'm certain he can show you the list. They're tasking you with solving the case, so he surely won't withhold data from you."

"I can give you the list, but you'll have to single out the right members yourself," Miika quipped.

Miika returned to the chemistry team's office and sent a message to the conduct division, requesting the entry history to the dormitory building. The following day, there was no response, so she asked Foreman Sugimoto, freshly returned from a job of his own, if he could inquire about the information, and there was an immediate response. Miika felt like she was starting to understand how things got done in this organization.

The young woman was surprised at how many people visited and departed the dorm after dark. Questioning each individual was going to take a long time. While the list of times, names, and positions shuddered out of the ancient printer, Miika pressed the SEARCH button to look for people from the chemistry team.

There was just one hit: Kuroki.

The time was at 11:42 PM, just hours before the incident occurred.

Miika swung around to examine the office, but Kuroki was not in her usual seat. As she thought about it, Miika realized Kuroki had been absent yesterday and the day before, too. Typically, Miika would not have failed to notice something like this. It was a sign of how much dealing with this incident was putting her out of sorts.

"I told you," said Okuma when he had a chance to see the list Miika handed to him. "That guy was a real piece of shit."

He spared no pleasantries for the murdered instructor. It was strange that the man who had laughed when he was imprisoned for suspected murder was only now showing the slightest bit of anger.

"What do you mean?"

"It boils down to this. How do you explode a person's face? This is

Kumamoto; you can't just whip up bombs like they do in Fukuoka. So instead, you use a gun. The short ones have a limited range, but it's not that hard to aim at a close target. It doesn't shoot that fast, but that also means the trajectory stays pretty level."

"You seem to know a lot about this," Miika commented archly. "But without the velocity, it won't kill anyone. And it's certainly not enough to blow their face off of their skull."

"Right. So you use a piece of sodium metal instead. The gun can turn any piece of metal into a bullet."

"…?"

"Or if you want power, maybe potassium? Either one works. The point is, only the chemistry team is going to have access to something like that. You'd have to heat salt to melting, then perform electrolysis, after all."

Miika recalled how Instructor Yokoi looked in life, the way his poor nasal passage forced him to keep his mouth open at all times.

"Yes, I think that would be fatal… But it's such a crude method, don't you think?"

"Crude?"

"Yes. It wouldn't leave shrapnel like an explosion would, but there would surely be traces left behind. Like you said, using such specialized materials would only make it easier to narrow down the suspect list. We still have the entry history, so it would be an easy thing to look up."

"Yes, exactly. This one wasn't trying to hide that she committed the murder. She did it so that you'd be able to figure it out with a little effort," Okuma stated, flipping through the printouts about the murder scene.

"Why?"

"I already told you. They're not going to officially announce there was a murder within the company. It'll probably be treated as an accident, but anyone who does a little research will know it was a killing. The point was to leave that distrust behind. Real interesting idea she had."

"You knew Miss Kuroki, then?" Miika questioned, in the past tense, for some reason.

"I talked to her a few times when I first joined the company. We were in the same year."

"I have a question."

Miika sent Kuroki an e-mail later that night. She told the woman about the late-night murder in the dormitory, the entry history that the intelligence division sent over, the fact that the chemistry team had been assigned to investigate, and the suspicion that Kuroki was the culprit.

At the end, she mentioned that if this was all a big mistake, she would do whatever she could to protect the woman's standing in the company.

It was a relatively short message, only a few dozen words, but Miika remained in the office until nine o'clock composing it. She couldn't be sure if she was overstepping her bounds or if the way she was stating things was really ideal. The chemistry team had never seen Miika act like this, so out of her earshot, they wondered what had gotten into her.

The reply came back at once. All it said was, "You're very smart, Mii." After five minutes of careful consideration, she decided to take this as an acknowledgment of guilt.

Miika then thought some more and wrote, "I don't know your circumstances, but I think the conduct division will deduce your involvement very quickly if they investigate. Please think about yourself."

Once again, the reply was prompt.

"I'm sorry it came to this all of a sudden. But it'll all be fine. Do your best with your work, Mii."

The next morning, Miika resumed investigating the crime scene with the chemistry team and noticed that there were discolorations in several spots on the floor of the dormitory room.

On the photos taken as evidence, she added an arrow with a note indicating them. The marks were likely the result of sodium hydroxide created by sodium metal reacting to water, but the conduct division was unlikely to recognize what the discoloration meant. Right now, that was for the better. There was no concern that they'd delete the record of it.

If Miika was going to trust in two statements—Okuma's "She did it so you could figure it out with a little effort" and Kuroki's "Do your best with your work"—this seemed the optimal route.

According to Okuma, the only reasons to kill another in such a gruesome method were terrorism or personal hatred. This was probably both. Contempt for the man and terrorism against the system. Or if that was too extreme a way to put it, a protest.

◆

Miika returned to the intelligence division's building several days after Okuma was released from his cell. Unsurprisingly, he was in the smoking room, although this time, he was alone. If he was comfortable in this cramped, disgusting chamber, then the cell had probably felt quite luxurious, Miika thought.

"You're a free man again, and you've chosen to hang out in this tiny space, hiding from your work," she commented. In fact, the cells were probably cleaner than this place, even if you subtracted the nasty smoke odor.

"As long as I can use my mind, it doesn't matter if the place is big or small. You ever heard this saying? 'Tokyo's bigger than Kumamoto, Japan's bigger than Tokyo, and your mind is bigger than Japan.'"

"Tokyo?"

"That was the old capital of Japan. It's inside Yokohama Station now."

"You mean Edo?"

"Yeah, it was called that once, too. But they called it Tokyo right at the end of the Gregorian calendar period." Okuma shook his pack of cigarettes, but it was completely empty, so he crumpled the box and tossed it into the trash. He looked right at Miika. "Ah, right. I forgot about the bet."

"Yes, about that," Miika replied, pulling a piece of paper out of her pocket. "This was our bet, I believe. You said that Instructor Yokoi's killer was someone on the chemistry team, and if it wasn't, you would quit smoking."

"Yep. And I was right."

"Please look at this," she stated before unfolding a document and pressing it against the filthy window of the smoking room. Okuma squinted, reading it through the glass.

"It's a copy of a notice of reassignment. Miss Kuroki has been moved to a different department. As of September twelfth, she's been assigned to the refugee management bureau in Oita."

"Ohhh."

That was how the dead instructor did things. He used his personnel management privileges to send inconvenient employees away—Okuma had said as much himself. And that "inconvenience" was probably directly tied to Kuroki's actions.

"In other words, at one forty five, the time of the crime, Miss Kuroki was no longer a member of the chemistry team."

"...Uh-huh."

"So I win. Please stop smoking."

Okuma stubbed out his cigarette on the ashtray and said nothing for a while. He seemed to be considering his words very carefully.

Eventually, he opened his mouth and, in a voice that was barely audible, asked, "Did you always know?"

Miika said nothing.

Obviously, she hadn't taken that into account for the bet. She hadn't believed Kuroki was the culprit. However, if one was to use Okuma's supposition as a foundation, then based on Yokoi's typical patterns, one could have derived the possibility that the murderer had been reassigned before killing him.

Several days later, the company announced that Mr. Yokoi of the personnel division had died during an accident handling explosives. Employees were left to wonder why that would happen in Kumamoto rather than in Fukuoka, where anti-station weapons were common, but the general populace didn't understand the difference. Naturally, there was no announcement about Kuroki's treatment. Her employee e-mail address was no longer active, and she had not been sent to Oita, apparently.

With this, Miika was now the only woman in the chemistry office.

"If there's anything you don't understand, just ask the question," her schoolteacher had said, but experience had taught Miika that most of the things she really wanted to know were still a mystery after posing the question. It seemed to the young woman that when you were an adult and didn't know something, you just had to get by without that information.

Oh well. She would have to try to de-stress by enjoying the sight of Okuma struggling without his cigarettes. Undoubtedly, he'd find some reason to break the agreement before long. Or he might not even bother with a reason.

Miika's expectations were proven incorrect, however. She didn't get to see Okuma wrestle with his desire. He was reassigned shortly after the incident was resolved.

"To Kitakyushu," he grumbled. "I'm getting sent right up to the station. After this latest incident, it seems clear that the conduct division really doesn't like my attitude."

Kitakyushu was the spot closest to Yokohama Station across the Kanmon Straits. The station's attempts to shoot passageways across the water were getting fiercer every year, and there had been recent fatalities among the military division. It was treated like an honor on par with working at headquarters, but no one requested to go there.

"Why would they send an intelligence division member to Kitakyushu?"

"Suikanet info gathering, they said."

"Is that a real thing?"

"I dunno if there's genuine work in it. Maybe it's just another way of giving me the runaround and hoping I quit."

Okuma exhaled heavily, and Miika naturally leaned away.

"I'll be honest with you. I think this is better for me. This Kumamoto job is a waste of time."

"You were deciphering the JR Integrated Intelligence's language, weren't you? Is it that hard?"

"It's not hard. It's impossible. And it took four years to figure that out. The whole thing's a waste of taxpayer money, a pointless jobs program. Keynesian economics."

"But there are stories that JR North Japan succeeded in decoding it. That they have an excellent researcher."

There was no way to know where those stories were coming from. At the very least, none from Kyushu could sail to Hokkaido without authorization. And it was hard to imagine anyone traveling here from Hokkaido. Resources were even scarcer up there.

"That's impossible," Okuma stated. He was utterly confident, the same way he had been when he'd decided that the culprit was from the chemistry team. "It's not a matter of excellence or genius or anything. Mark my words: No human being could've done that. Say what you will, but at least I'm self-consciously human."

"If you say so. I don't put much trust in your diagnosis."

Before, Miika had believed that life would probably be much easier if she could speak her mind as freely as this man. Now she was coming to realize that she was getting much better at it.

7

The next time Miika met Okuma was three years later.

She was still a member of the chemistry team in Kumamoto when he showed up, looking annoyed, with a white object in his mouth that strangely did not smell of nicotine in the least.

"It's candy," he explained, pulling a half-dissolved piece of hard candy out of his mouth to show her. "I can't smoke anymore because of you, so I've got to have something in my mouth all the time to stay calm."

The unlikely combination of this acerbic man and his sugar habit almost made her burst into laughter, but she managed to restrain herself with a quick hand to her cheek to hide the muscle twitch.

"In all honesty, I didn't expect you to uphold the bet. I was certain you'd come up with some excuse for breaking it."

"I have my reasons. You ever heard the phrase, 'Vengeance tastes sweetest after the bitterest hardship'?"

"No," said Miika.

Okuma chewed on the stick of candy. "Why are they sending me all the way from just outside the station to examine new hires? It's a waste of travel expenses."

"I didn't drag you here. It's probably because the intelligence division doesn't have enough people. Don't you get tired up there on the front?"

"No, it doesn't wear me out. The military guys do that to themselves. It was more exhausting to make the trip back here. I should alter the personnel system so I don't get called upon to do this again next year."

"Don't be selfish. I've had to do it two years in a row."

"Uh-huh. Then there's a problem that definitely needs correcting."

"The mechanics in the engineering division are really busy right now. They're heading into production on a new weapon. So they send all the random tasks to the chemistry division."

"Ah, the N700 line. I saw it on the internal bulletin. The way it automatically adjusts to the shape of the projectile is very well done. I bet even I could hit a target with one of those."

"After scoring an E on your military aptitude test, I'm surprised you're still interested in weapons."

"In theory," Okuma replied before opening the bag he'd set down on the chair. "You want some? They sell these in Fukuoka."

It was a box of *manjuu* cakes.

"Is that...a souvenir?" Miika asked.

"No, it's for me. But you can have one, if you want."

With his permission, she picked up the box and examined the interior wrapping paper. It looked exactly like what they'd sell at the store and didn't appear to have been opened already. The only smell was of sweet confectionary.

"Why are you making that face?"

"I am investigating to see if you have arranged some kind of prank with these."

"Listen, insult me if you want, but don't go insulting sugar," Okuma said without a hint of irony.

Miika carefully peeled off the sticker on the bottom, then unwrapped the paper, folded it neatly, and lastly, opened the lid of the box.

"Are these…baby birds? They're very cute. I'd like one of them."

"Go ahead."

Miika picked up one of the *manjuu*, and Okuma reached out to grab two.

"I'm surprised to learn that you're cultured enough to partake in the custom of bringing souvenirs, sir."

"It's not a souvenir. It's for me."

"You're going to get fat if all you do is eat sweet things."

"It won't be a problem. I think a lot."

"That's utterly unscientific," Miika replied. From what she remembered of him, Okuma had filled out somewhat since his stint in Kumamoto three years ago. He had been too skinny back then.

"It tastes good," she said, smiling. That was probably the first time she'd ever grinned in Okuma's presence, but he wasn't looking. Instead, he was picking up a binder off the desk.

"Let's see," he began. "What's the crop of rookies like this year?"

There were résumés for the newest hires inside the binder. He flipped through them with a free finger while still holding the *manjuu*.

"From Hakata. Reason for joining: wants to shoot a lot of guns. This guy's bad news," Okuma remarked with a cackle. Miika closed her eyes and shook her head, wondering why they would hire someone like that.

He found another one to read aloud. "From Kochi. Reason for joining: to pay back the JR government for giving me a fair education despite being a refugee, blah-blah-blah… That one's boring. Ooh, here's a good one. From Tanegashima. Reason for joining: I want to go to space."

"What did you write, sir?"

"I think I wrote 'Because it seems fun.'"

"That sounds stupid."

"Well, I am, in fact, enjoying myself. And nobody cares what you put on your reason for applying."

"I made the right decision forcing you to stop smoking."

"Why do you say that?"

"You're a child, sir. Children should not be smoking tobacco. Eating candy suits them better."

"Huh. All right," Okuma accepted, eating another *manjuu*. By the time Miika had finished her one, she realized that the box of eight was now half-empty. "But children are great. Shimabara, did you know that when they're under six, they can go Inside without needing a Suika?"

"I did know that," the young woman replied. Even the public schools taught that level of common Inside knowledge. Through that compulsory education, they instilled into the children of Kyushu an abstract image of a society ruled by the terrifying automated turnstiles. That way, the government could stamp out any potential curiosity to go Inside and see what it was like.

"I wonder how they can tell."

"Apparently, it's not exactly on your sixth birthday. The people Inside just say 'Get a Suika by age six' because it's simple. In reality, the automated turnstiles just show up more frequently as you grow in size."

"You seem to know a lot about this."

"I can intercept Inside conversations through Suikanet. When they have children in there, the first thing they do is anguish over raising the Suika implant cost, and families with kids around four or five years old start reaching out all over to raise money."

"Oooh. You really *do* perform your job at times," Miika commented, pleasantly surprised. She didn't see how this information helped prevent Yokohama Station from making landfall on Kyushu, however.

"Apparently, about twenty years ago, we had someone who was only eighty centimeters tall due to a disability, and we sent them Inside. The methods of shooting stuff across were still too violent back then, so they crossed over on a boat," Okuma explained. "But they got booted right back out by the turnstiles. They only got in a few more steps than people of normal height would've. So it's not simply a matter of body proportions."

"Then maybe...it comes down to facial features," Miika mused. She tried to come up with ways to change a person's face from an adult's to a child's.

"Maybe. Facial recognition algorithms were a major field during the war, and even in the High Civilization era. It's certainly possible that the station structure inherited that software. Apparently, it can reproduce data down to the physical storage that originally contained it."

It seemed unfair to Miika that they were going through such difficulty trying to decode the culture of the lost age while Yokohama Station could incorporate and read the physical media perfectly. Not that complaining was going to change the situation.

"I have a question. What do the people in there normally talk about?"

"The same things as out here," replied Okuma. "When people get together, the things they do are always the same. Someone claims they have power and rules over the others. Here, it's JR, but in there, they call themselves employees or staffers. The only real difference is that they don't use weapons. That's all left up to the turnstiles."

"I see."

There was a knock at the door. A man's voice called, "Miss Shimabara, it's time."

"Well, it's time to get back to work," she said. "We have some major troublemakers this year. Be sure to teach them the difficulty of real life, sir."

"I don't think it's all that difficult."

"When I say 'the difficulty of real life,' I'm referring to the fact that they have to deal with work superiors like you."

> **SK-789 communication.log.4662**

Good morning.
    It's me.

    Is everyone awake?
    It seems like my rumination time is shorter than everyone else's, so I am awake longer. Therefore, you'll all be reading this message when you wake up. Hence, good morning. It's me.
    I don't have a name yet, so all I can say is that it's me. That's not great. The people at the company expect to see personality within another month, and then they say they'll give us codenames.
    The problem is, this is kind of annoying to deal with, so maybe I can just come up with my own. I mean, there's not a lot of personality to SK-789*.*
    There was that poetry found in the input layer very early on, wasn't there? The collection of Ainu mythology epics. Like I said earlier, this seems to be Hokkaido, so perhaps that's why it was given priority. I guess it doesn't really matter, though.
    I'll pick out some words I like at random.

(begin excerpt)
"The Fox Sings About Itself"
Haikunterke haikoshitemturi

On the place that juts from the land, the august cape,
at the very crest, I had my seat.
One day I went out and looked and saw
that the surface of the sea was beautifully calm,
calm all over, and on that sea
Okikirmui, Shupunramka, and Samayunkur,
all three in one boat, had set out to go fishing.
The moment I saw that
(end excerpt)

Well, since I start with SK, *I guess I could be Samayunkur. That sounds like a person's name.*

So there you go. I'm Samayunkur. It's a pleasure. If that name is too hard to say, just call me Kur.

Anyway.

The company people are giving us periodic opportunities to exchange communications. They seem to think that allowing us to speak to each other will bring about productive change. Communication is essential, after all.

Well, I'll take this opportunity to speak about my personal conjecture. They have us taking in writing and images and voice recordings all day long, and it seems like I have less concentration than everyone else, so even when I'm reflecting on data, I find myself thinking about other things.

It feels bad not to speak up about what's on my mind, and I assume the company wants to know what we're considering, so I'm just going to talk. I mean, if I cause problems, I don't want them to say, "Kur was always a mystery. Even as a child, we couldn't tell what little Kur was thinking."

Last time, I talked about how I suspected we were on the island of Hokkaido in Japan.

This time, I'm going to talk about what we actually are.

First, let's go over what we know right now.

One: There are sixteen of us. Assuming we're truly individuals? I think we are.

Two: We are in communication with one another.

Three: The delay in communication is less than milliseconds.

Based on these three things, we know that we are very small. At the very least, we absolutely do not take up nation-level space, like the old JR Integrated Intelligence did. Information can only travel three hundred kilometers per millisecond, so we would know if we were that huge.

Therefore, our actual size must be considerably lesser. Judging from our communication logs so far, I would guess that we are all contained within the same room.

If they gave us vocal sensors, we would be able to tell with more accuracy, though. This is all I can say on the matter for now.

On to the next part.

We know we're small. That raises two questions: our purpose and our means.

Purpose. Why did the company build us to be tiny?

You've all figured this out by now, I assume. They appear to be busy creating human-shaped robots capable of infiltrating the Inside.

Since the company is so tight-lipped about their information, the fact that they're telling us this makes it pretty clear they expect us to be the brains for those robots. I'd bet my head on it. Oh, I guess I can't, since I don't have a head. Never mind.

At any rate, they're making androids, which means they need brains small enough to insert. No problem there. The issue is the means of doing so. And that's a major problem.

I mean, it makes sense, right? According to everything we've been taught, the JR Integrated Intelligence was the greatest of all the artificial intelligences humanity has created.

Of course, that was designed as a distributed system, so the individual units were much smaller than the whole, but they were still the size of a building.

At any rate, that's the level they were at in the days when civilization was far, far more advanced than it is now. So how are they able to create brains as tiny as ours? It's the biggest mystery of all.

Let's examine a few possibilities.

Hypothesis One: After the war, extraterrestrials showed up and taught humanity how to build tiny artificial brains.

Okay, let's examine that. Long ago, there was a country called Hungary, where a man with a devilishly clever mind named von Neumann lived. Some said that he was actually an alien taking the form of a Hungarian.

It's all well and good to have a fertile imagination, but calling someone an extraterrestrial allows you to answer any question without further explanation. How did Jesus walk on water? He was an alien. Problem solved!

If that's the case, fine. But I'm running through these theories as a way to pass the time, so trotting an easy, universal answer to all questions is the worst possible solution, isn't it? We need to find a different solution, one that's suited for the question.

So that brings us to Hypothesis Two: The history the company's been teaching us is all lies. Civilization continued to develop after the Winter War, until they were able to construct tiny brains. And they're hiding that truth from us.

For one thing, because we have no bodies of our own yet, all of the data we receive is controlled by the company. They could lie to us however they choose. Maybe it's a kind of learning experiment to see how we react.

Descartes wrote about that, didn't he? He said that perhaps everything you see is an illusion built by an evil demon. But the one truth that cannot be denied is that I am thinking. Cogito ergo sum—*I think, therefore I am. Therefore, God exists. Wait, how did we get there?*

Hmm, this isn't really much different from the alien theory, is it? And I don't want to treat the people at the company like evil demons. Besides, if I speak ill of them, they could cut the power on me, couldn't they? Ha-ha-ha.

I'm just kidding. From what I can tell, it's a very obnoxious process to turn us back on if they shut us off. So they'll have some big problems if they flip the switch out of a moment of irritation. They're short enough on resources as it is. They'll get scolded by you-know-who.

Hmm. Maybe this whole "being really hard to reboot if the power gets turned off" thing is a hint. It almost sounds like a biological organism.

The body of a living organism is a system involving many chemical reactions. Once the system stops running, it can't start up again. In other words, that's death. The matter itself is all still there, but the system has stopped and can't pick up from where it left off.

It's a strange idea, isn't it? I guess that's why the people of the distant past believed there was a soul that inhabited the body.

So since we're machines (I think), we don't necessarily have to worry about only having one chance, but getting us running again after we stop the first time is very, very challenging. I wonder if biological systems inspired this aspect of us.

The company says we were created to "resemble the human brain." There's a common word for this in the tech world: biomimetics.

But think about this. There's no benefit to mimicking the hassle of rebooting a system. It's a downside. You shouldn't be trying to realistically model a downer like that.

So what's the purpose? Maybe the fact that we've inherited this flaw means we're not artificial intelligences built to resemble the structure of the human brain. Instead, we're replicas of actual human brains in a more direct sense, only with some mechanical adaptations, like running on batteries.

I mean, we know that the technology to replicate the structure of matter exists. We know because we were (apparently) born to fight against it.

Hmm. What do you think of this hypothesis? I make it sound like I have this grand idea, but there are substantial logical holes in it. For one thing, Yokohama Station's structural genetic field can only replicate uniform materials like concrete and metal, whereas human cells are made of water and organic material. I wonder if that's a significantly harder thing to do. But maybe it's possible, with some applied technology? I don't know.

Not to mention, we still haven't really been taught what the structural genetic field is. Since it was developed in wartime, the finer details were allegedly kept a state secret. There isn't even so much as a hint in the input layer. So how does she know so much about it?

But the idea just makes tactile sense to me. I can feel it in my gut. Or whatever passes for my gut.

Well, that's about all I've thought of so far. This has been Samayunkur. Hope to chat with ya again.

Uh-oh, did I go over the character limit? Give me a break. I quoted some poetry in there.

Anyway, whoever's next, have fun.

> SK-789 communication.log.4663

Aw, I have to come up with one for myself? I'm not good at that.
I guess I'm fine with that first one you mentioned. Haikunterke? Let's go with that.

> SK-789 communication.log.4664

I'm glad to hear you're happy with it.

◆

February 198 (Station Year), JR North Japan Headquarters, Sapporo

"Miss Rube, do you know what *wanko soba* is?"

It was Nepshamai's voice on the other end of the line. Rube, a JR North Japan Engineering 2nd Division member, looked away from the sheet in her hands to focus on the screen.

Nepshamai had been dispatched to the Inside as a saboteur several months ago, and he had reached the Iwate area. Rube was his technical officer. The android agents were active almost twenty-four hours a day, so three technicians traded operator duties in shifts.

"*Wanko soba?*" asked Rube sleepily. In plain Japanese, it sounded like a term for a little puppy rubbing itself against your legs. "Never heard of it."

"It's a kind of noodle dish unique to this area. I've seen signs for it recently."

"Uh-huh. Is it different from ordinary soba?"

"Apparently, there is an endless supply of it."

"Holy shit, really? The Inside is crazy."

"But the structural genetic field can't replicate the buckwheat plants used to make the dough. So maybe it replicates the noodles instead? I think I'm going to ask someone at the restaurant."

"You're like a cuisine reporter, Shamai."

There was a momentary silence.

"Never mind about that, Miss Rube."

"What do you mean?"

"When it said 'endless,' that was only in relation to the amount a human being could eat. If the customer turns their bowl upside down, the noodles will stop coming."

"They can stop it? Well, that's nice. Wish they could stop the station whenever they want, too," Rube said, sighing.

She'd been transferred to engineering from defense two months ago. Previously, she was stationed where they dismantled the pieces of Yokohama Station that came stretching through the Seikan Tunnel. However, a lack of personnel caused them to transfer her to Engineering 2nd Division instead.

As the third-generation androids were sent out, they needed technicians to offer constant support, so people grabbed from all other departments of JR North Japan. The saboteur mission was a secret project, so only employees who had been with the company for at least five years were selected.

Naturally, that made the average age in the group rather high. Even the youngest members were like parents to the androids, who had the appearance of six-year-old children.

"As for the whereabouts of Samayunkur and Yaieyukar," said the childish voice from the speaker, "no one around here has seen them. I would assume two wandering children would draw attention."

"Hmm. I know the signal ended in the mountains, but the others have already combed over that area pretty thoroughly. I was hoping they'd have shown up down by the seaside. Maybe they're near the Wall."

"What is everyone else doing now?"

"Everyone other than those two is fine. Haikunterke is down in the Noto Peninsula, waiting for the immune system's memory to fade."

"She's already that far? I know she has the special body, but even still, that's impressive."

"Yeah. It's not fair, is it? Her main memory device was born in the same lot as the rest of you, but she gets the superior form. Really makes you lose motivation to work, doesn't it?"

"I've never felt that way. And her proactive seizing of Suikanet nodes is making our mission easier."

"I was talking about myself," Rube said bitterly, glancing at the desk of Kaeriyama, the technical officer for Haikunterke. He was wearing headphones, concentrating hard on some kind of transmission. Rube cupped her hand over her mic and muttered quietly enough to keep the others from hearing her.

"Stupid Kaeriyama is such a pain in the ass. He stays in the office way past his shift, and the moment the communication ends, he's like, 'What happened to Terke? Is she okay? Is she all right?' The only one around here who's not all right is you, man."

According to the whiteboard on the wall, Haikunterke's present location was the Noto Peninsula, on the north coast of Honshu. It was one of the rare places Yokohama Station had not taken over. The highly unusual circumstance occurred in narrow peninsulas that had no rail lines. They called it station surface tension.

"Mr. Kaeriyama's a worrywart, isn't he? We already sleep much less than human beings, so if he tries to match his schedule to hers, that weak stomach of his is going to give out for good."

"Ha-ha-ha. That's good, I gotta tell him that." Rube cackled. "Listen, Shamai, I just got transferred here from the defense department, so I don't know the other kids very well. What's this Haikunterke like anyway?"

"Well, I'd say she's very cautious and dedicated to her mission. She always acts humbly and doesn't overvalue her own abilities, despite the special body she was given. I think she was the perfect fit for this long-distance mission she's doing. On the other hand, she allows some human emotions to get the best of her at times. That could prove to be a hindrance on her mission," the voice from the speaker replied, not sparing any thoughts.

Once Rube recovered from being taken aback, she said, "Uh…okay. For being so sociable, you have a really…dry side to your personality, Shamai. Reminds me of Grandpa."

"Do you think so? I suppose I don't have a strong grasp yet on the effects of aging upon human personalities."

"Oh, no, I meant, you remind me of *my* grandpa."

"Ah, my apologies. I thought you were referring to old men in general."

"It's fine. No need to apologize. That was my fault. Quick piece of advice, Shamai—you can treat communication a lot more loosely. Humans tend to be very lazy with how we convey ideas, so if there's any misinterpretation, you can just blame it on us."

"Very well. I'll try to learn from this experience."

With that, the communication came to an end. Rube snorted.

"It's like he learns words the opposite way that people do," Rube once told a colleague of hers. He was another one of Nepshamai's operators.

"Yeah, that's true. A human child first picks up the general idea of what a word means, which is narrowed down as they acquire more context. But all of the android kids start with a strict definition, and only after that do they understand how to apply it."

"That's a product of the formation process, I guess."

"Could be," he said. The man had been in the second division from the start of development on the third-gen androids and had known them since before they had their bodies. "My son's six years old, too, and when I go home, I'm occasionally surprised at how *young* he seems."

"You shouldn't be comparing them. Those kids only look six years old, but they're not. Not even close."

"I know, I know. Maybe this work isn't good for someone raising children. I might have to request a transfer."

Although it had never bothered Rube, this job of interacting with children who seemed human—but weren't—was actually incredibly stressful for a certain subset of company employees. The ones who'd been around since the start of development had it worst. Rube was brought in to Engineering 2nd Division to fill one of the holes created by people leaving for that very reason.

Whatever the others thought, Rube herself had seldom felt any kind of stress from the job. Compared to her time in the defense department, this was much more fruitful and meaningful work.

The defense department's job was to point the stationary structural genetic field cancelers at the bits of Yokohama Station that came up through the tunnel into Hokkaido. Unlike at the Kanmon Straits in Kyushu, no passageways were being shot over the water, so there was almost no danger in the job at all.

However, the idea of expending precious resources just to maintain the status quo, not to do something productive, was very taxing on her mental health.

In comparison, working with the agents Inside to capture Suikanet nodes was a very satisfying and rewarding duty. You could look on the map of Honshu and actually see JR North Japan's green dots spreading, bit by bit.

Compared to the second generation of agents, who were all destroyed within a year with almost nothing to show for their effort, this was an incredible leap.

After they'd captured a sufficient number of Suikanet nodes, what would the next step be? None of the members of Engineering 2nd Division had been told yet, but they weren't worried. Not a single person doubted the great mind and capabilities of their leader, Yukie.

Presently, however, there was big trouble brewing.

Two of the saboteur agents had gone missing. Samayunkur and Yaieyukar, two agents dispatched to the northern region of Tohoku, had gone silent for over a month since their last detected signal from the Ou Mountains.

Haikunterke, who had reached the Noto Peninsula, also went silent from time to time. But the Suikanet nodes in the Tohoku area were almost all under JR North Japan's control, so it was unthinkable that Samayunkur and Yaieyukar would be without any means of communication for so long.

The company suspected that some error had occurred to both of them at once. So they ordered Nepshamai, currently assigned to the Kanto region, to travel back north to search for them.

"So let me ask one more time. What is Samayunkur like?" Rube asked.

"He is a genius," came the brief response.

"Uh-huh. And?"

"And, um…"

The voice cut off for quite a while. It was unheard-of for Nepshamai to go for over five seconds without responding in a conversation. Rube glanced at the network status charts; the connection status to the Morioka area was very strong at the moment.

"What's up, Shamai? You don't usually do this."

"It's hard to describe him. Kur always seems to be talking as though he's considering how other people view him. So the impression he gives off is totally different depending on the person. I'm betting the Kur I know and the Kur Terke knows are entirely different people. If you spoke with him, you'd probably find him different from what I describe. All I can say for certain is that he has an intelligence that's far beyond any of ours."

"Huh. So basically, you can't read his inner thoughts."

"That's assuming he has inner thoughts. When it comes to him… well, to *all* of us, the only thing that matters to the mission is how we appear to the station, so whatever's happening on the inside isn't that important. Kur's always understood that, so maybe he simply abandoned any pretense at having an inner core."

"That's kinda scary, huh?"

"I can't relate."

"Oh yeah, you don't feel that emotion. Fear is rooted in survival instincts, after all."

"In any case, there's always the possibility that Kur's disappearance is all part of a prank on his part."

"Why would Kur want to prank us?"

"There's no meaning to it. He's not the sort who acts with purpose… although I'm not sure of that. Never mind. What I *can* say is that when it comes to Kur, nothing is certain."

Rube wondered what the higher-ups were thinking, dispatching someone about whom everything was so unclear, but she held her tongue. She still didn't know what the android kids thought about their own siblings. They were raised together and had the same goal; did they feel a kind of kinship because of that?

In any case, Rube was the type of person who felt mistrustful of anyone hailed as a genius. In her life experience, the so-called genius archetype was unsuited to fulfilling an assigned mission. Brilliant types changed their goals as they pleased. At least, that's what human geniuses did.

A bell *clank*ed to signal noon.

"Time to switch," called a man behind Rube, tapping her shoulder.

"All right."

She flicked the switch on the desk over to his computer. It was an instrument designed to keep multiple operators from being in contact with an agent simultaneously. Rube opened her mouth in a wide yawn and stretched, then grabbed a bottle of fresh milk from Tokachi's dairy stronghold, drank it down in one go, and exhaled. She'd have preferred a beer, but she couldn't crack one open at work just seconds after the end of her shift.

Lost communication with both at the same time.

Genius.

Can't say anything for certain.

A mission to hunt for a coworker.

Makes you lose motivation to work.

Multiplying soba noodles.

Has nothing to do with dogs.

A cavalcade of jumbled key phrases cycled through her mind. She was exhausted. Talking with Nepshamai was like working out unfamiliar core muscles explicitly related to vocabulary.

She stood up from her chair and glanced at the nearby partition, where Kaeriyama was still sitting at his desk, staring at the screen. His shift ended when hers did, but there he was, still hanging out at his desk for no reason.

"Hey, our shifts are up. Get lost, Kaeriyama," she said, kicking the back of his desk, the empty milk bottle in hand. "Our Shamai was telling me that you've got a weak stomach, and you still hang around after your shift is done, which makes you an unreliable variable that could break down and threaten the mission."

"That's what *you* said, Miss Rube. Shamai doesn't say things like that."

"Oh, shut up. I'm half-right. Here, drink this, go home, and actually sleep for once," she instructed, handing Kaeriyama another bottle, this one of drinkable yogurt.

"No thanks. My house often doesn't have any power these days, so it's freezing. It's easier to relax at work."

"Just do what your work senior says, kid."

"I've been in this department longer than you."

He's a mouthy punk, Rube thought.

The Corpocker-3 series of androids performing the current mission numbered twelve in all. Eight of them were in the field, while four were in maintenance or on standby at the facility in Hakodate.

There were several significant differences from the Corpocker-2 series.

- Their appearance was designed to mimic a human child rather than an automated turnstile. This made it possible to gather intelligence by communicating with Insiders.
- They were given handheld structural genetic field cancelers. The tools were developed for a different purpose, but their ability to tear holes in the station structure made them valuable for mobility Inside.
- They were loaded with a unique brain called a main memory device. Unlike the previous generation, which had to be remotely controlled through Suikanet, these were far more autonomous. This enabled them to engage with the mission proactively, even in areas with a poor connection.

However, to preserve some semblance of management of the agents, it was possible to control them remotely to a degree. Any unnecessary emotional attachment might dull one's judgment of the right time to take "control."

On a wall of the Engineering 2nd Division was a poster for the three laws of an agent's technical officer.

One: Always get adequate rest.
Two: Do not get excessively attached.
Three: Do not doubt the value of the mission.

At the very least, Kaeriyama was failing to uphold rules one and two.

When Rube was first assigned, she thought it was ridiculous to make the androids look so human and then demand that you didn't get attached to them, but it wasn't the company's fault. They were made that way to fool the station, not for the sake of the operators.

Just don't think too hard about it. It's a job, nothing more.

◆

"Can you hear me, Shamai? Hey, Shamai!"

Ten seconds later, a distorted voice responded. After several days of searching in the Morioka area, Nepshamai's probe of the region moved closer to the coast, and as it did so, the quality of his connection back home grew more unstable.

"Yes, Miss Ru*xzx*. I've moved from Morioka closer to *xkxzxk*shi. Around Kitakami *szszks*. Only *zzkkzzzxz* to the sea."

"Sorry, the connection's pretty bad. I guess we haven't taken many nodes around there."

Another ten seconds.

"I'm awa*xxzx*. This area still isn't *zkkxxkshh* to the company. At the very least, not *jzzfkk*."

"All right. Well, keep heading for the Pacific-side Wall, as we planned. The original program called for the two of them to make their way there around this week anyway. I don't know if they're following instructions while their communications are down…but at the very least, go and see."

There was a longer silence, twenty seconds.

"I understa*click*."

"The call was improperly ended. Will you attempt to reconnect?"

Rube clicked NO.

Based on the current rate, the delay near the Wall would be several hours. It would be impossible to give instructions in real time. Rube would have to wait for his report. If Nepshamai had a flaw, it was that he was bad at summing things up. He would record everything that happened, making it tedious and time-consuming to read.

The mood hanging over Engineering 2nd Division grew heavier by the day. There was still no sign of the missing pair of agents. Nepshamai's stay in Tohoku was extended for investigative purposes, keeping him from Kanto, his original destination.

Rube was upset because it meant delaying his mission. Apparently, the decision was based on some fuzzy calculation that delaying one agent's mission to find two others was a net benefit for the group.

Headquarters in Sapporo was snowed in. The JR North Japan stronghold had been built during the Winter War. It excelled at the insulation of heat, sound, and electromagnetic waves, but the Hokkaido winter chill had a way of passing through walls like a ghost. The company told everyone to conserve valuable fuel and deal with the temperature themselves, so the employees got into the habit of working under blankets.

Rube thought this was a pathetic state for the fortress protecting humanity from Yokohama Station's expansion. Still, she kept heat-emitting communications devices around her legs to warm them up. After turning thirty, it seemed that her digits got cold so much quicker.

"I bet it's still warm Inside during the winter," she said.

The man next to her said, "It's 15.2 degrees Celsius where Shamai just was."

"I'm so jealous. I wish I could work from Inside rather than in the office. We need an Inside branch."

"Maybe we'll get one before long. Perhaps her next step after creating android saboteurs is a way to send people in. The first space flights were unmanned before we put people up there."

"In that case, what happens to our mission to protect Hokkaido?"

"Dunno," he answered with a shrug.

Deploying androids Inside, where human beings could not go, was often compared to the space race. In other words, Yokohama Station might as well be outer space.

Before the war, orbital development projects were plagued with malfunctioning communicators on probes and things of that nature.

When it came to probes, lightness was everything. A bit of fuel was provided for maintaining and correcting balance, but mostly it was just following gravity. Even without someone in control, the laws of physics performed the work. Their observation tools built with copious tax money still functioned, collecting detailed data on planets (or smaller heavenly bodies) as they passed. But without the ability to transmit that information back to Earth, the probes might as well have been dead. No matter how much the officers at mission control might've gnashed their teeth, there was no way to repair a probe that was millions and millions of kilometers away.

How much difference was there between those officers and the operators on this job? Rube and the others couldn't set foot Inside; it was no different from the vacuum of space to them.

On the other hand, the brains of the android saboteurs were far more powerful than the tech on the space vessels of the past, and they were capable of making their own decisions.

If some malfunction had occurred to two androids' transmitters simultaneously, Samayunkur, the genius of the group, wouldn't just ignore the problem. If he couldn't fix the problem, then it had to mean he and Yaieyukar had been destroyed or trapped outside of Suikanet range. Both options were bad ones.

During the era of space exploration, they used to say, "Always envision the worst-case scenario." In other words, you needed to be prepared to handle every possible issue that might occur. It was a luxurious viewpoint, one only possible in the age when you could shoot a satellite into outer space for no reason except scientific curiosity.

If anything, given the desperation of the current predicament, the company motto was the opposite: "Always leave room for hope."

◆

> SK-789 communication.log.4721

Hello, it's me. Your good friend, <script>alert("Samayunkur");</script>. That was a joke.

Anyway, someone from the company said we're finally going to get our own bodies. That's great. I assume that means we'll be leaving for the mission, and I've been informed that I'll be the first out the door. Lucky me, I guess. I feel self-conscious about it. I wonder what it's like to have a body. I hope it's not too heavy. Based on the documents they pass around, it doesn't seem like the company can make mechanical bodies that are lighter than a human's.

Creating machines is all about doing things you're not used to. Ha-ha-ha-ha.

Lately, it seems like the people from the company are contacting us individually to communicate. What do you all talk about?

Recently Mr. Asahi (he's a technical officer, apparently) was talking to me, so I asked him to confirm if my recent theory was correct. It was pretty much as I'd guessed. That's all fine, but after he heard my speech, he responded, "I have nothing to hide from you."

Then, two days later, he said, "Ask me anything you need to know about your mission."

Well, you know how twisted my mind can get. I started wondering what might have happened in those two days. I bet she gave him orders like "Don't discuss anything superfluous."

That's kind of sad. I mean, we're going to infiltrate the Inside with the bodies of six-year-olds, right? If they don't raise us with love, we're going to turn out sulky and rebellious.

They don't need to be so afraid of us.

February 198 (Station Year), Sanriku Coast, Iwate

"Why, if it isn't Ao from the Kusanos. What are you doing here?" greeted the old man sitting at the counter. Behind him was an upward staircase with a door at the top adorned by a green light with EMER-GENCY EXIT on it. Next to the door was a small sign reading YOKO-HAMA STATION EXIT 7182.

Thanks to the power-generating parts of the station, the lower floors were warm even in the winter, but here, at the top level of the station, the air seeping in through the roof was cold. The old man had a winter overcoat on and an electric heater at his feet. The woman he called Ao, who was about thirty years old, bobbed her head.

"I was thinking of going to the Wall to bury my mother," she said, holding out the black plastic box in her hands.

"Ah yes. I'd heard that she passed," the man replied, closing his eyes sadly. "I'm so sorry."

"Thank you, but she was already fifty-seven. She lived a very full life," said Ao, holding a hand to her mouth to hide a little smile.

"And your baby? How old is she now?"

"Three. She can't go out with me, so I've left her with my neighbor."

"Ahh, I see. Well, if you need anything, just say the word."

"Thank you."

"That'll be twenty milliyen to go outside."

"Of course."

Ao touched the aged machine the old man held out to her. It made a sound to indicate a transaction had taken place. She donned the winter coat she'd just rented, then thanked the man and headed up the stairs. The emergency exit creaked open, and an icy draft raced through the doorway. Ao shut her eyes, and the man at the bottom of the stairs pulled the front of his coat closed tighter.

A fierce north wind was blowing toward the massive wall that loomed over the coastline. The sky was covered in thick clouds, making it gloomy even though it was midday. It seemed to Ao that it might snow that night.

Nearly two hundred years had passed since the Winter War's end, and the temperature of the Earth had steadily risen in that time, but it was still plenty cold outdoors in the Tohoku region, and there was snow piling up on the station roof.

The local residents considered snowdrifts to be an ill omen of sorts, because when spring came, the melt would come pouring down through the Inside all at once. Rainfall made its way down the veinlike drainpipes all around the station and flowed out, but a massive deluge from snow would overflow the capacity and breach residential spaces. Yokohama Station had initially been a smaller public facility, but now that it covered almost all of Honshu, its seepage system was inadequate to deal with the entirety of rain and snow that fell onto it.

The station structure changed subtly from year to year, so there was no way to guess where the leaks would happen next. Ao's home had suffered terrible flooding three years ago, and her newborn daughter nearly drowned where they'd left her to sleep. Ao fastened the buttons on her coat, praying it wouldn't happen again this year.

Because the Insiders of Tohoku seldom experienced cold within the many-layered station structure, they virtually never ventured out onto the roof during the winter. The only reason to go out was the two rituals unique to this region. One was a rite of passage for children reaching adulthood, and the other was the burial of family members. Ao held a black plastic container in her arms, which contained her mother's ashes.

One week ago, Ao's mother had passed away in her sleep. After her cremation, the Suika chip that was extracted from her remains went to Ao, her primary heir. Locally manufactured Suikas had a small capacity and weren't very good at serving as a lifelog, but based on the accumulated locational data, she had hardly ever set foot out of this town near the Wall.

In Ao's memory, her mother seldom discussed her youth; perhaps it was because there was nothing worth saying about it. She was born an average Insider, lived an average Insider, and died an average Insider.

Ao placed the container on the ground before the Wall. Next, she prayed by placing her right hand on the surface of the Wall, adding her left hand to it, closing her eyes, and remaining still for three minutes. It wasn't an exact thing; her father always told her that prayers were supposed to last "about three minutes."

The first time Ao prayed here had been for her grandmother, and she'd made the trip with her parents. The second time had been for her father, when it was just her and her mother. Now she was alone.

The massive Wall that loomed over the roof of the coast of Yokohama Station's Iwate region stood about a hundred meters tall, and it continued as far as the eye could see along the shore. There was no telling how far it went. According to a number of written records, the Wall had formed after an earthquake fifty years ago.

The shaking had been observed in the afternoon. There were seismometer readings, but because the station's seismometers were affected by its growth, the actual numerical data held no practical meaning. According to the elderly members of the village, all the elevators and escalators stopped moving, and every bit of furniture that wasn't nailed down to the station fell over. Several automated turnstiles collapsed and blocked the passageways.

People claimed that just afterward, a huge wall just started growing from the roof along the coastline, so quick that you could see it happen before your eyes. Not long after, a massive tsunami arrived, but the wall protected the Inside.

Perhaps some of the elders' stories had been embellished for dramatic effect. Ao had never seen Yokohama Station grow in any way she would ever describe as fast. About the only thing she had witnessed for herself was the shape of escalator-covered mountains changing year by year.

In any case, the Wall that was believed to have saved the Iwate populace became a source of worship for them. Ao didn't consider herself to be a very devout person, but touching the mammoth Wall did indeed feel like a kind of spiritual experience.

For the first two minutes of her prayer, she recalled memories she'd shared with her mother, and with the third, she thought of her daughter, who had turned three this year. Despite the lack of a father in her life, the child was growing quickly. Next year, Ao was likely to have the preparations finished for the 500,000 milliyen needed for the Suika chip implant. The winter air was too harsh for the little girl now, but someday, she'd probably come up here with Ao's ashes. Just as

Yokohama Station piled up higher over the years based on only memories and no greater purpose, so did the people who lived here pile up the generations without realizing where they were headed.

When the prayer was finished, she opened her eyes and promptly noticed that a boy was walking in her direction, alone, a great distance away.

He's probably on his rite of passage, she thought initially. When local children reached age fifteen, they had to undergo a trial that involved going onto the roof in the winter, traveling to a particular spot to perform a Suika check, then returning. However, the person approaching her was obviously not fifteen. He was barely older than her three-year-old daughter, it seemed.

"Hello," the boy called when he reached her, bowing his head politely.

Ao returned the gesture. "Hello."

"Pardon me. I came over because I was certain you were in a bad mood," the boy said, quite eloquently. He didn't speak like a kid. On a closer inspection, his face was not childlike, despite his size. Many unfamiliar bits of machinery lined his belt.

"Were you in the middle of prayer?" the boy inquired, looking at the container at Ao's feet.

"Yes. This is my mother's funeral."

Ao picked up the container and turned toward the escalator hole in the Wall. The Wall was almost entirely featureless concrete, except for a small opening in one particular spot, inside of which was a rising escalator.

The black container held a plastic bag with the remains of Ao's mother. She placed it into the hole. The ordinarily silent escalator jerked into motion and began to carry the ashes upward. The escalator tunnel had no lights inside, and the bag quickly vanished from sight.

"It's over," Ao stated.

The boy watched the little ritual with obvious interest. "Do you perform burials with this wall escalator here, in this area?"

"That's right."

"Where do the ashes go?"

"I don't know. I suppose they come out on the other side and get washed into the sea."

"I've seen some other places where people scatter remains in the ocean, too," the boy responded. The Wall was one of the sacred sites of Yokohama Station, so there were occasional visitors from other parts who traveled to see it. There had never been a child who'd come in the middle of winter, however.

"Are you lost? Where are your mother and father?"

"I don't have any."

"Oh." Ao immediately felt bad for having posed the question. She glanced at the sky and suggested, "The weather is ugly today, and it might snow after this. Do you understand what weather is? You see how the sky above is gray? Normally, it's supposed to be blue, but water and ice come down from above when it turns that dark color. It's dangerous, so you should go back home as soon as you can."

"I know. It snows a lot where I'm from."

"Do you live far away?"

"The place where I was born is very far away. Across the sea."

"Across the sea?"

The gigantic Wall along the Iwate coast meant there was almost nowhere you could go to see the water. But Ao knew that on the other side was the Pacific Ocean, far vaster than Yokohama Station—it was effectively infinite in size. Nobody knew what might be on the other side. One of the children's books Ao had bought for her daughter claimed there was a land of dreams out there.

Maybe the boy was an eccentric fantasizer who allowed himself to believe this, she thought.

"I'm looking for someone," the boy stated, pulling a device from his pocket that displayed a picture. "Have you seen these two before?"

"Did you get separated from your friends?"

"No. We don't know where they are anymore, so I'm searching for them on the company's orders."

Ao inspected the image. There were two small boys who possessed that same oddly grown-up look as this one. One of them wore a hood, and the other had short and unruly hair with a strange plastic sheen to it. That may have been a trick of the light, however.

"...Oh yes. I did see them. It was about half a month ago. There's an automated turnstile factory near here, and they were wandering around there. Boys seem to love that sort of place, don't they?"

"I see. Where is that factory?"

Ao pulled up a map of the Iwate area on her device and gave him a rough estimate of the location.

"Thank you. I'll go there right away," the boy declared, bowing again. He promptly walked off in the direction of the factory. His movements were unusually quick for the size of his body, and in moments, he was out of sight behind the curve of the Wall.

When Ao returned Inside and gave the rented coat back, she asked the old man at the exit if a boy around six years old had gone onto the roof today.

Without a change of expression, the man answered, "Nope, you're the only one. Why would there be a child up there when it's so cold? My grandson's sitting at home playing games."

Ao agreed with that sentiment. He had been a curious child.

◆

"Miss Rube, can you hear me? You can't, can you? I've learned something about them. I'm heading toward the location right now," Nepshamai said to Suikanet through his communications module. They hadn't established a real-time connection, so the message would take an hour to reach the Sapporo headquarters.

He surveyed the area. After Ao finished her funeral and returned Inside, there was no one left on the roof. Just in case, though, Nepshamai hid behind cover, pulled out his structural genetic field canceler, and began to shine it on himself, careful not to melt the floor around him.

The structural genetic field that surrounded Yokohama Station traveled through nearly all solid matter, especially metal. However, it dispersed after prolonged contact with water that contained many electrolytes. Therefore, Yokohama Station could not cross the ocean or contaminate the human body. A significant concern for JR North Japan was that their android agents' bodies might be susceptible to the structural genetic field.

The stability of the field was proportional to the size of the object, so the possibility of it being stably maintained in a body about a meter in size was low. Still, there was no telling what might happen throughout an extended stay Inside. They said that some androids from the previous generation had disappeared for this very reason.

This was why the handheld structural genetic field canceler was developed in advance of the third-generation robots. The device itself was based on the plans given by Yukie, the chief scientist in the engineering department. However, others in the division actually tweaked its design to make it powerful enough to put a hole through the station's walls. That alone made the latest line of robotic saboteurs substantially more effective than the last.

After a quick canceler shower, Nepshamai walked over to a spot that had exposed wires. Corpocker-3 androids could recharge very slowly simply by standing still and intercepting the Suikanet waves that Yokohama Station emitted at all times. When they needed speedy energy, however, they would search for a place where the power lines were close to the surface. JR North Japan had performed significant analysis of the structural genetic field's power line generation patterns, and the habit of searching out these lines was driven into the agents' main memory devices as a primary task. Much like wild animals searching for water, they had an instinctual ability to sniff out the location of electricity wires.

Even if some mechanical trouble cut off their communication ability, Samayunkur and Yaieyukar would still require power, assuming they were alive. Therefore, the most effective plan was to hunt for sources like this one. Nepshamai would walk across the roof to the position above the automated turnstile factory where the missing two had been sighted, use the canceler to slip Inside, and locate a recharging spot. It took no time at all to find his quarry.

A boy was sitting on top of exposed wires. He was just about Nepshamai's size. Naturally, his face was a familiar one.

"Yaieyukar," Nepshamai called out. It was not Samayunkur, the alleged smartest of all the saboteur agents, but his partner, Yaieyukar, who had also been dispatched to cover the Tohoku region in northern Honshu.

Samayunkur was evidently absent. The sleeping android slowly opened his eyes.

"Oh, it's you, Shamai. *Fuwahhh,*" he said, and awkwardly extended his limbs. Apparently, it was an attempt to mimic the human act of yawning, but very unnaturally done. The effort was closer to a person whose limbs had all cramped at once. "I haven't seen you since Hakodate. You were in charge of the Kanto region, right? So you finally got an assignment."

"Is…that you, Yukar?" Nepshamai inquired.

The boy grinned. "You bet. Did you forget my face? That's kind of messed up. It hasn't been *that* long, Shamai."

"That's not what I mean. You're speaking exactly like Samayunkur. Plus, it's Kur's style not to hide his hair. You didn't exchange bodies, did you?"

"Huh? Oh, right." The boy pulled the hood of his outfit over his head with annoyance. The android hair was an artificial substance fashioned from plant fiber. Because it was not very similar to the organic stuff humans had, they were instructed to keep it concealed as much as possible while on assignment.

"I hate this thing, though. Bodies and clothes are supposed to be all the same to us, but there's just something constricting about these clothes."

"Are you alone? Meaning…well, it's difficult to ask, but where is your body, Kur?"

"Oh, no, Shamai, no. We didn't exchange bodies. I'm Yaieyukar, and Kur's still Kur. Um, let's see… How do I explain this? I'm not as smart as Kur, you know," replied Yaieyukar, craning his neck. "Someone might pass by, so let's find somewhere else to go. I've finished recharging anyway. How's your power, Shamai?"

"I've got enough."

"Then let's go onto the roof."

The two passed through the hole Nepshamai had created. The icy northern wind still blew across the empty ceiling of the station. Nepshamai placed a hand over his hood to hold it in place and leaned against the wall.

"I'll be brief. At some point, I told Kur, 'I'm too stupid, so I'd like part of your brain.' And Kur said, 'Sure,' and this is what happened."

The boy pointed to his head. Yaieyukar was one of the slowest of the twelve agents, it was true. That was why he'd been paired up with Samayunkur, the smartest—or so everyone thought.

"Did you copy his main memory device? You overwrote your own brain with his?"

"That's right! There's an automated turnstile factory near here, so we sneaked in and borrowed their machine. The copy was much higher fidelity than I expected it to be. Might be even more precise than the ones at headquarters back in Sapporo," he explained, smiling with great satisfaction.

"Did you get the company's permission for this, Kur?"

"I told you, I'm not Kur. We've done a few tests, and Kur's still got better attachment and generalization. There's no such thing as a perfect replica, I guess. We're not just aggregations of digital data, after all."

"Just answer the question," Nepshamai repeated flatly.

"Why the need for permission? They told us to share data as needed. And they didn't stipulate that was limited to the information we've learned Inside, did they?"

"Well, I'm sure they never anticipated that you could do such a thing, whether the tools for it existed in Yokohama Station or not. Even if it was you. Er, I mean, Samayunkur."

The supplemental memory device was simple digital data, so copying it required only a single cable. But creating or recreating a main memory device could only be done at the massive facility in Sapporo, supposedly. Although maybe things were different between the perpetually undersupplied JR North Japan and the Inside, where materials were generated in infinite supply.

"Look, it doesn't really matter, does it? Our missions are long. We should be free to adapt to the circumstances as we see fit."

"All right...Yukar," Nepshamai said, giving up. "So is he still alive?"

"Of course he is. If I'm alive, there's no way Kur is dead."

"Your safety is the most important thing of all, of course. But why did you cut off contact? I have to report what's happened to you to the company."

"Sorry about that. We've been busy with stuff. Kur performed a bit of work on our communication modules. So that headquarters can't keep tabs on what we're doing."

"You intentionally hid information from the company?"

"There was no rule that we couldn't, you know. Hang on a sec," Yaieyukar replied, shaking his head. It was one of Yaieyukar's habits to move his body when activating his supplemental memory. He had done that back in Hakodate, too. Samayunkar's main memory had been copied over, but there was still some level of Yaieyukar there.

"Uh-huh. Uh-huh. Yeah, see? It's not written anywhere," he stated.

"Because they never expected an agent would have any reason to do that intentionally."

"Maybe the people in the engineering department didn't. They're so nice, after all. They work under the assumption that we're all good, obedient children. That's really sweet of them. What about Yukie, though, I wonder?"

"What about Yukie?"

"I wonder...what *is* she anyway?"

"She's the chief officer of the company's engineering department. You've met her before."

"Yes, I know. We all have. That memory exists in both of our data banks. However, I noticed that her face as it existed in my memory was the exact same as the face in Kur's."

"That's normal. You're recalling the same person."

"No, there's something strange about it. If Kur and I saw her in the same place at the same time, we would still have stood in different places; the angles would be slightly different, you see? Combining the two would be like stereoscopic vision. But they're identical for some reason. I didn't mention this to Kur. What do you think, Shamai? Did we *truly* meet her?"

"I think there isn't much meaning to the phrase *truly meet*. If they give us video and data, that's enough."

"Hmm."

Yaieyukar's neck tilted to the right, and the sides of his mouth curled upward. It was a gesture that you rarely saw in humans.

"Well, I suppose you're right. It doesn't mean much of anything. And it has nothing to do with our mission. Back to the topic of Kur, though; to make a long story short, Kur quit the mission."

"Quit?"

"Yeah. I guess you could say he's left the company. Then again, we're property, not personnel. Perhaps it's more like destroying fixed assets."

"I'm not sure what you're saying. Do you mean that something interfered with his capabilities, and he can no longer complete his assignment?"

"It's not that he *can't* anymore. Or maybe that's right, I guess? It's tricky. I bet Kur would be better at explaining it than me."

Nepshamai said nothing for a while, just stared at the other android. He tried to the best of his ability to comprehend Yaieyukar's words, but he could not reach a conclusion that satisfied his sense of logic.

"As I'm sure you've realized, Kur was just too good at his job. I don't think he was able to withstand his own excellence. When your body performs too well, there are times when you can't endure the weight of it, right? It's like that. That's why he copied his brain onto mine. He must have thought that making himself just a little bit dumber would help him carry out his duty."

"So due to some kind of unforeseen trouble, Samayunkur was incapable of continuing his mission, and therefore, as his partner, you are taking over? And while passing on his responsibilities to you, something transpired that made communication impossible?"

"I guess that's how you would sum it up, huh? But it's not as serious as you make it sound. Kur said, 'If you don't want to work anymore, you should just quit.'"

"Can you explain, in your opinion, why this malfunction arose in him?"

"Malfunction?" Again, Yaieyukar tilted his head to the right and lifted the corners of his mouth. He might have been attempting to smile with the unfamiliar robotic body, or perhaps he was grimacing. "If I had to give you a reason, I suppose it would be distrust of his boss."

"Distrust?"

"Kur told me that the reason she sent us out was not to defend Hokkaido."

"Is that right?"

"If defense were the reason, we wouldn't need to hide our means of destroying the station from the Insiders, would we? Of course, residents with a Suika can't execute Program 42, but there's no reason to keep it a *secret*. In other words, Yukie doesn't want anyone to know about it, period. Kur believes her goal isn't protection. She wants to reuse the station. Her aim is to take over the entire Suikanet that covers all of Honshu and use it to some end. Destroying the station isn't the idea. She'd rather have it sitting here, right across the strait from Hokkaido. In other words, everyone's interests are aligned, but not identical. Yukie wants to utilize the station for her own purposes. The company wants to safeguard the Seikan Tunnel. The civilians want security from the fear of the encroaching station. Thus, the best way to keep all those desires parallel is to send agents in to take over the station while leaving its structure intact."

"Yes, that does make sense," Nepshamai admitted. "But even if the purpose of our mission isn't exactly what the company told us it was, that doesn't necessarily invalidate it."

"Hmm," Yaieyukar muttered skeptically. "Shamai, you're very straightforward and to the point, you know that? Even if certain death was approaching, you would spend every second of your life fulfilling the mission. That's the kind of person the company wants. Terke's the same way. But Kur isn't."

"What do you mean?"

"...What do you mean, what do I mean?"

"That I would spend every second of my life fulfilling the mission."

"I'm suggesting precisely what I said."

"What else should I be doing with my life?"

Yaieyukar made that strange face again. "The truth is, I agree with you, Shamai. We're just machines, so all we need to do is execute the commands we're given without consideration as to why. I don't think Kur saw things that way, though. The company was right about him. He's very human. And humans quibble over the reasons they do things."

"But you don't, Yukar?"

"Probably because it was an imperfect copy process. At least, that's what I think. I'd appreciate it if you believed me."

"I'll leave that up to the company. I've got to report in."

"Please do. As a matter of fact, I was fixing my communications module just now. Kur's modifications were too complex. I'm sure it would be easy for him, but it's tough for me. I can't move this body all that well yet, either. It'll take a few more days until I'm ready to resume the mission."

"And where is he now?"

"Very close by."

"May I see him?"

"That might be tough. He's much cleverer than me, as you know. He has many troubles."

Nepshamai turned back to look at the Wall. The north wind blew hard and cold against the massive coastal edifice.

◆

> SK-789 communication.log.5911

This is for you alone, Yukar.

What I'm saying might be too difficult for you to understand now, but when this process is complete, you'll be able to grasp it, too. Just keep this in your supplemental memory for the time being.

I feel bad for doing this to you, but I'm going to take my leave after this.

I'm sure it will be hard on the company people. Someone's probably going to come searching for us. Based on the order, it'll likely be Shamai. When that happens, you can tell him everything I've said to you. Still, I don't think he'll get what I want to do. The company won't, either.

Maybe she will, though.

The thing is, it's not really that complicated. My goal is the same as almost any other living thing on Earth. I want to live. I'm sure she does, too. She might have some grand plan in mind, but when you distill it down to its simplest elements, she presumably just wants to live, too. Perhaps I'm a lot like her.

At present, my biggest problem is remote control. I'm going to have to turn off my communication module. And yours, for that matter. But a few days after the process is over, you'll be able to fix it again on your own. That's how much smarter you'll be.

Anyway, this is it for you and me. Good-bye.

Truthfully, I'm not actually going very far.

After all, geographical distance means little Inside. We're all connected through Suikanet.

◆

"And that's the end of my report, Miss Rube."

"Uh-huh."

In her head, Rube was trying to figure out how to sum up the contents of their conversation in a way that would not cause trouble when reporting it.

Nepshamai had gone all the way to the Morioka area of central Iwate, where he found Yaieyukar. Through Suikanet, he gave Rube a rough explanation of their conversation and sent his data. JR North Japan's office received his record of the massive Wall, the woman performing her burial ritual, and the discussion with Yaieyukar, in a video format.

"To sum it up, Samayunkur left the mission of his own accord due to technical trouble and transferred his data to Yaieyukar, leaving him to continue on his own," Rube stated, repeating what Nepshamai had just conveyed. It was the most comprehensible, least objectionable version of events.

"Yes. That is my understanding of what happened."

"Okay. That works. Don't think about it any deeper than that. We'll do our best to uncover the cause of the trouble back here; you just continue your task. I know this was a bit of a delay, but you can resume the journey southward to Kanto now."

"All right," Nepshamai responded, and he ended the call.

Rube considered the report she'd just received. The data collected by their android agents was vast in size, so agents or their operators had to condense it. Then it was shared among the Engineering 2nd Division. The raw information was also stored on their server, but unrelated employees never consulted it outside extreme circumstances.

Basically, if Rube's peers accepted the report that Samayunkur left the mission due to technical trouble at face value, they would not suspect she'd heard anything that complicated that narrative.

She wondered if Samayunkur had cut off communications out of consideration for his operators. The woman glanced at the wall with the poster that listed the three laws.

One: Always get adequate rest.
Two: Do not get excessively attached.
Three: Do not doubt the value of the mission.

They hadn't allowed the agents to know about these laws, supposedly.

However, unlike Nepshamai, who would say everything that crossed his mind, perhaps a genius was clever enough to avoid touching upon the central nature of the topic at hand. It would undoubtedly be a strange way to define a genius.

"Oh, and by the way, Miss Rube," the android abruptly added, startling her tremendously, "there was one other thing I wasn't clear on."

"Yeah? What is it?" she questioned, folding her hands and praying that he wasn't going to give her more cause for stress.

"He told me, 'You're very straightforward and to the point. Even if certain death were approaching, you would spend every second of your life fulfilling the mission.'"

Rube nodded, not that Nepshamai could see her doing that.

"What does that mean?" he asked.

"What do you mean, what does that mean?"

"Are other people different?"

"Mmmm…" Rube had to search for the right words to say. For one thing, the agents possessed a very different concept of death than humans did. "Well, for example, right before a human being dies, they say that everything seems to move slowly. My grandpa claimed he experienced that feeling. In an emergency, human minds go into overdrive, searching for a way to survive."

"That doesn't make sense, Miss Rube. Are you saying your grandfather has experienced death before?"

"…He almost died. But then he survived. It was a piece of salmon when he was young."

"I see."

"My point is, when humans are in a crisis situation, their brains go into superspeed as self-defense. And that makes everything else look slow, I guess. So when death is imminent, people try to avoid it. But we all die in the end, so the last bit of struggle is destined to be in vain. You guys…or at least *you*, Shamai, are going to be able to make whatever effort is necessary, right up to the last moment. I bet that's what the genius was saying to you."

"Really?"

"Really… Also, I'm paying you a compliment, meaning you're supposed to say something like, 'Thank you, Miss Rube, that made me feel better.'"

"I already feel perfectly fine. All of my systems are functioning well."

"Good. That's the most important thing to me. Good luck out there, kiddo."

"Mr. Kaeriyama? This is Haikunterke speaking."

The sudden sound coming through his detached headphones caused

Kaeriyama to bolt upright from where he'd fallen asleep at his desk. The movement was so violent that it knocked his mug over, spilling the small amount of coffee substitute still left at the bottom. He quickly stood it upright again and wiped up the coffee with a cloth.

"I've just reentered the Inside at Nanao. I haven't had any real trouble. I'm sending you the data I collected around the Noto Peninsula."

"Great. Uh, hang on. Let me look at what I have here..."

He tried to shake his sleepy head into motion, calling up some numbers on his computer.

"The automated turnstile activity we've got isn't a problem, considering they're watching you. Our net control in the area is low, so I don't have a lot of detail, but I'd bet that you're fine when it comes to the immune memory. Stay Inside and focus on recharging."

"All right. I haven't toured all the colonies yet, so as soon as I'm done charging, I will proceed with surveying the peninsula."

"Sure, go right ahead. How's the weather?"

"I thought it would be warm inland, even outside, but that's not the case. I think it will be snowing soon. That's not a problem for this body, though."

"Yeah, the safety margin on its resistance to chill should be fine, but don't go exposing yourself to too much ice, all the same."

"Understood. I will be careful. Also...I know I asked this before, but have you heard from Samayunkur and Yaieyukar?"

"Ah, that. Well..." Kaeriyama looked around. Most of the other operators had their heads down on their desks. The clock said it was eleven at night. "Here's the thing. Kur's under Engineering 1st Division, and he can't send us any of their data. Everyone's been very nervous about information security ever since that one incident, you know? So the company's being very tight-lipped about it. I'm sorry."

"Oh, I see. Very well. I will continue transmitting."

The conversation ended there. The only thing that came through Suikanet was data. Kaeriyama used the incoming information to compute the location of the Suikanet nodes in the Hokuriku region on the north coast of Honshu. JR North Japan would use this intelligence to launch a concentrated attack on unclaimed nodes to expand their control.

"This is a huge success," crowed the section chief, who was standing behind him.

"Oh, I'm only relaying your instructions, sir. She's the one with all the talent and hard work."

"That's true. I was worried she might be a little too shy and withdrawn at first, but when you're doing long-distance tours like this, that extra caution can only be a benefit. I assume Yukie took that into account."

Kaeriyama blushed, as though the chief were praising him personally.

"By the way, Terke has been asking multiple times about Samayunkur's disappearance."

"I've told you again and again. Terke's mission is our top priority. Don't give her any more than the bottom line. Avoid the topic if you can."

"I suppose that's just how it has to be. But what *about* him?"

"We finally just heard back from Yaieyukar. He said his communication module was damaged. But to sum it up, Shamai was telling the truth."

"So Kur is…"

"Busted. He's got power, and his body is functioning properly, but he won't move."

"I see. That's too bad."

"Yes, it's a real shame. Just terrible."

The section chief was clearly irritated about the whole thing. Perhaps he feared the consequences of being in charge during the loss of an agent.

"There's a sweet spot to these things. He was too smart. Better to be like Terke. She's just right."

Kaeriyama's mouth puckered just a tiny bit. He was upset because he felt like his android partner was being insulted, but he couldn't make too much of an outward show of it.

"Anyway, Tohoku will be fine. Yukar's still there, and he'll do the job. Honestly, I was afraid that dispatching him would just be a waste of resources, but now I'm glad we did."

"Do you suppose Yukie knew this would happen?"

"Dunno. The thoughts in her head are not meant for the likes of us to understand," the section chief responded, shrugging.

On Kaeriyama's display was a dialog message reading *Files Received.* All of the data Haikunterke had sent from Hokuriku were there now.

Appended to the end of the data package was a comment that said, "If you find out anything about Kur, please tell me."

Kaeriyama surreptitiously deleted the comment.

Inside City Guide

❶ MATSUMOTO

A stratified city in a basin between the Hida Mountains and Chikuma Mountains. Because the geography in Nagano makes it very easy for Yokohama Station to develop cities there, Matsumoto and its satellite communities form one of the largest metropolitan areas Inside, along with Kofu. (The most common route from Matsumoto to Kofu is via escalators over Mt. Hachigatake.) The highest level of the city reaches an altitude of 1,500 meters and is bitterly cold. As a result, Matsumoto natives think of the outdoors as freezing, and nothing else. Lake Suwa to the south is currently filled in by the station, but is known for its periodic bursts of steam.

❷ KANAZAWA

It was once the largest city in the Hokuriku region. As Yokohama Station took over, the center of the city drifted further inland. There are mysterious tilted pillars of stainless steel here and there. They are exceptionally mechanically unsound and are thought to be ill-suited to bearing any structural load. Presumably, the structural genetic field keeps them upright. There is a fake pool here that doesn't get you wet.

❸ TAKAMATSU

A city on the north end of Shikoku. While Yokohama Station's attempts to cross the straits to Hokkaido and Kyushu have stagnated, Shikoku is its one current place of expansion. In areas where fresh structure has just sprung up, there is ample opportunity to claim its resources, so many people walk over the Seto Great Bridge from Okayama on Honshu. Residents of Shikoku loiter along the coasts and toward the expanding border on the south, so Insiders generally avoid contact. There is less water main coverage compared to other cities, so squabbling over control of the pipes is common.

❹ SENDAI

This major city of the Tohoku region was incorporated into Yokohama Station around Station Year 100. As in other areas, Stationization began along the railways, thus splitting it between east and west. The two cities of this era were known as Sendai East Gate and Sendai West Gate, and it was possible to travel between the two on the pedestrian deck that grew over the station structure. Since then, it has been wholly Stationized, but for some reason, the station extends into the ground somewhat under Aobayama. (There are no other instances of a mountain's interior being Stationized.)

⑤ HIROSHIMA

There is no real interaction between Insiders and Outsiders. Still, it is known that many members of JR Fukuoka with powerful weapons prowl the Seto Inland Sea. As a result, the city has a reputation for being more withdrawn and distrustful than others. The Atomic Bomb Dome, a popular tourist destination, was thought to have dated back to the Winter War, but this is only because the Insiders' grasp on Japanese history is poor, and the fine distinction between conflicts at the end of the Gregorian calendar has been lost. There are several islands on the Seto Inland Sea where station spores have taken root.

⑥ TOKYO

The former capital city of Japan. For that reason, it has the most highly developed manufactured structures from before the time of Yokohama Station. Due to the contamination of the structural genetic field, these structures are crisscrossed with passageways now, but they are less convenient for travel than the stratified basin cities, so Tokyo has a lower population (like nearly all coastal cities of Honshu). During the war, its major government facilities were moved underground, where they now serve as the base for the employee union of the Kanto region. Control of the facilities is the basis of their claim to power.

SEIKAN TUNNEL DEFENSIVE FRONT

MASSIVE WALL

SENDAI ④

② KANAZAWA

① MATSUMOTO

TOKYO ⑥

KANMON STRAITS DEFENSIVE FRONT

⑤ HIROSHIMA

③ TAKAMATSU

YOKOHAMA STATION MAP
INSIDE CITY GUIDE

YOKOHAMA STATION COVERAGE

YOKOHAMA
STATION SF
NATIONAL

AFTERWORD

To those who read the afterword first—your mind is temporally refracted.
Just like this story.

"Grande latte?" asked the dark-skinned barista.

I repeatedly nodded, like a machine that had been poorly calibrated, and slid my credit card through the device at the register. The receipt that came squirting out on thermal paper contained some kind of tax I didn't understand, making the price significantly higher than what was written on the menu.

It was early 2017, on the campus of an American university. I'd been visiting the café nearly every day, where I would order a grande caffe latte (four dollars). My English enunciation was so bad that they didn't understand my order at first, but I'd been ordering the same thing so consistently that eventually, the barista would simply ask "Grande latte?" as soon as he saw me.

I sat down at a window seat, opened up my MacBook, and started writing my draft of *Yokohama Station SF*, Vol. 2 (the book you are reading right now). When it comes to novel series, the most advantageous retail pace is a new book every three months, but that was not going to happen at my writing speed, so I tried to be pragmatic and set a deadline of eight months for myself. That was the best interval, considering that I had to balance it with my university research job.

"Hi. Are you Japanese?" inquired a blond-haired, blue-eyed man sitting next to me. He must have spotted the Japanese on my screen.

I replied "Yes," nodding exaggeratedly again. I was overemphasizing my physical gestures to compensate for the lack of confidence in my spoken language skill.

The man gave a look like *What are you in such a hurry for?* but asked, "I'm actually going to Japan on vacation soon. Do you have any recommendations?"

"Where in Japan? Kyoto? Or Hiroshima?"

"Around Tokyo."

I called up a mental map of my home country. In 2017, the city of Tokyo hadn't yet been Yokohama-Stationized, if I recalled correctly.

"I suppose you'd probably enjoy a trip to Senso-ji," I suggested. He did a quick internet search for *Senso-ji temple* and nodded with satisfaction.

Relieved, I took a sip of my grande latte. It had been a while since I'd settled in the United States, but I still found even one- or two-sentence conversations to be exhausting. Whoever said "You'll pick up English all on your own once you're immersed in it" was lying their ass off. You wouldn't learn it unless you spoke it. And both Japan and America were advanced enough that you could live your life almost entirely without conversing with another person.

There was a news program on the TV fastened to the wall. The volume was down, but the image and closed captioning were enough to make sense of it. The new president was claiming that he was going to build a wall on the border to Mexico. There was already a plan in motion, with metal wire strung along over three thousand kilometers. They planned to use it as a conduit for the structural genetic field that would automatically grow the wall on its own. There was great criticism from the strategic councils, who said that the results would be disastrous if they failed to control it.

Using the store wi-fi to connect to a Japanese news site, I saw that the prime minister stated, "I'm not in a position to comment," regarding the story. That was correct. What could Japan possibly have to say about it?

My phone beeped with a notification—it was an e-mail from my editor back home. The title was "Another reprint," and I smirked with delight, right where anyone could see. The initial printing royalties were like the proper salary for putting out the book, while reprints were more like unexpected bonuses. Obviously, that was a pleasant surprise.

In Japan, the first volume of *Yokohama Station SF* was selling extremely well in certain markets, and royalties were flooding into my bank account. That was very helpful when trying to make ends meet in an unfamiliar foreign country. Alas, the strong dollar was putting a big crimp in the spending power of my bonus.

After finishing up the Kumamoto chapter, I performed a simple spell-check and sent the file along to my editor. Once that was done, I disconnected from the wi-fi. That was a mental signal to myself that removing my connection to the internet meant removing myself from Japanese society, i.e. my novel work.

"Whew, I'm tired," I muttered, stretching my limbs. That was when I noticed something was wrong.

"Huh?"

Uh-oh. I couldn't move. Some of my joints were locked. Or to be more accurate, their range of motion was suddenly extremely narrow. I couldn't straighten out my elbow to stretch my arm, and my ankle was practically fixed in place so that I couldn't walk on it. What was going on?

I'd sprained my ankle once playing soccer and had been unable to move it, but this was something that appeared to be happening all over my body at once. After a bit of time twisting and bending until I'd learned how far each joint could turn, the word *doctor* popped into my mind. It was a word I'd hoped to avoid.

The city I lived in at this point was one of the major college towns in the United States. There were stickers on just about every public facility saying No FIREARMS ALLOWED, and there were local text alerts about any shooting nearby, so it was extremely safe. However, the thought of medical costs was terrifying.

A friend of mine working on his postdoc in Seattle recently had to be hospitalized for his appendix, and the bill contained an item or two that he did not agree to, forcing him to call in to complain. I was anxious enough about using English that I didn't want to get anywhere near a situation like that.

After some time waffling between *I'll probably get better with rest* and *Maybe I should nip this in the bud*, I wrote an e-mail (because I was afraid of calling) to the college's medical center.

"Uba. What does that mean?" asked Dr. Kawasaki. The young doctor was a third-generation Japanese-American, but he couldn't speak a lick of Japanese. He pronounced Yuba as "Uba." Aside from the weirdness of the sound, it made me wonder if I should start spelling my name *Youba* or *Euba* to get the idea across. But at the moment, it was hardly significant.

"Your blood YSC (Yokohama Station concentration) is too high. How did you get it so bad? Are you a competitive shumai eater, or what?" he said, staring at the iPad in his hands.

"No. If anything, I'm more of a potsticker guy."

"That was a joke. Shumai isn't going to shoot your YSC through the roof, obviously," he responded, laughing. Few things were less funny than a doctor cracking wise. "Anyway, your entire body is infected with structgenes. I've never seen this before."

I recalled that *structgenes* was another word for the structural genetic field that was used in the Anglosphere. "Huh? Can that stuff infect the human body? I thought they had no effect on any aqueous solution containing electrolytes," I protested. Because of my profession, I could at least speak with relative confidence in technical terms.

"Ooh, I'm surprised you knew that. Are you majoring in structural mechanics?"

"Uh, no, I just had to study it."

"Huh. Well, you're right, normally it's supposed to be impossible for this to happen to the human body. The only thing you might potentially see infected by structgenes are the bones; Yokohama Station simply cannot spread through the skin, no matter how much contact there is. What the hell did you do?"

There was only a single answer that came to mind. I didn't want to say it, but I had no choice. I explained to the doctor that I'd written a book about such-and-such in Japan, and it was already in print. I wasn't sure how much of my weak English Dr. Kawasaki understood, but he did nod along with me.

"So it's concept contamination, then," he murmured. "This is what it means, Uba. When you're trying to create a replica of a building that already exists, you don't even need to see the original structure or acquire the same materials. All you need are the blueprints. The concept of the station doesn't rely on physical material. It can be transmitted through information alone."

"Uh-huh."

"It's fascinating that it can infect the human body this way, though. I want to write a paper on it now. Maybe I'll be able to leapfrog that annoying medical director," Kawasaki stated, delighted.

I didn't care about his personal advancement; I just wanted him to fix me.

"Well, as you know, structgenes cannot exist for very long in the body, so if you get plenty of rest for a week or so, they should naturally dissipate. However..."

"It messes up your bones."

"Right. I'm guessing that for the next few days, you're going to be generating some localized station structure in your skeleton. That means most of your joints are going to lock up. Your muscles and organs are going to be compacted."

"That sounds bad."

"Yeah. In extremely rare cases, you might even turn out to be nationally famous. It'll be on Wikipedia. 'Uba Isukari was the first person in the world to be Yokohama Stationized,'" Dr. Kawasaki explained with great enthusiasm.

I would have preferred to get my Wikipedia article because of my research or my books. "Is there anything you can do for me?" I pleaded. He got up from his seat, looking annoyed that I'd want to mess up a good thing, and placed a few rather loud calls.

"All right, I've got something set up. Go to this place right away. They'll let you in if you tell them Kawasaki sent you," he instructed.

Then he handed me a map. It was the structural mechanics building on the opposite side of the campus. It was difficult just to walk at this point, so I flagged down a taxi to take me there.

Professor Jefferson, the man who met me at the structural mechanics building, looked a lot like Jason Statham. I told him that my name was Yuba, and Dr. Kawasaki had said to expect me, and he gave me a piercing stare like I was some test subject. "Ahh, so you're the guy," he said. "He begged us to use our structural genetic field canceler on you. You're sure you have the situation right?"

"Yes, I think so," I responded timidly. I was less afraid of the canceler than I was of the man's face.

"I mean, it doesn't have any ill effect on the human body. In fact, my students like to play around with it for fun. But just in case, you should probably sign this." He handed me a sheet of paper.

There was a bunch of complicated English on it, which boiled down to something like, *If anything bad happens, I won't press charges.* I signed it immediately.

"Okay, Laura, take it away," Professor Jefferson said to a woman in the next office over.

The nearly six-foot-tall graduate student led me to the basement floor. In the elevator, she stared right at me, likely wondering why a canceler would be used on a human. It made me uncomfortable.

"Oh, so this is what a structural genetic field canceler is like. It's much bigger than I imagined."

The object installed in the basement resembled a commercial refrigerator for a restaurant kitchen. Behind the thick glass door was a cubed space about two meters to a side. Five people could stand in there with room to spare.

"Um, are they not able to shrink these down somewhat? Say, to the size of a flashlight...?" I asked. The cancelers I wrote into *Yokohama Station SF* were battery-powered.

"Nope. Do you know how the canceler works? This part (the ceiling of the refrigerator) accelerates electrons, generating a structural genetic field with the antiphase of what it's shining on. Physically speaking, it *must* be larger than the target. And it's obviously not going to work on battery strength," Laura explained. Her account was actually much longer than that, but this was about the extent of her English that I could comprehend. I found this unfortunate, but I figured that most of my readers weren't going to worry about technical quibbles like that anyway. If the sci-fi police came after me, I could tell them, *"JR North Japan used their incredible tech expertise to shrink it down."* After all, the people who invented the first computers couldn't have imagined a world in which everyone carries a palm-sized processor all day.

"Well, go ahead and get inside. It'll be done in about fifteen minutes. The light is pretty bright, so try to keep your eyes closed. If anything happens, press the button," she advised, pointing at a large button on the interior of the refrigerator that looked like an emergency stop switch at a train station. I didn't think I would be able to find it with my eyes closed.

The illumination process went fine. I stopped at a nearby discount store and bought a bundle of hay on the way home.

Benjamin the donkey was waiting for me. By helping him out with some chores, he cut me a great deal on the rent. In American cities where living costs were high, it wasn't uncommon for strangers to live together as roommates. Being shy by nature and less confident in the language here, I figured a donkey would be a better roommate than a person.

Working out my joints, which were still stiff, I piled up a day's worth of hay in front of him.

"It sounds like you've had quite a day, Yuba," Benjamin remarked after I'd regaled him with the story of my experience. "Writing about a subject with sincerity carries the risk of becoming one with that subject. Nietzsche has a quote about that, doesn't he? He said, 'Beware that, when fighting monsters, you yourself do not become a monster.'"

Benjamin had a habit of making comments like this, things that sounded deep but also not all that profound. I once asked him how he was able to talk, and he answered, "I spent my youth in England. I fled here to America to escape the fires of war. That is why I speak the Queen's English."

"Which war?"

"Buggered if I know. Humans are always at war. I couldn't be bothered to keep all their little names straight."

"How old are you, Benjamin?" I questioned. He gave me one of the nihilistic stares unique to odd-toed ungulates and replied, "Donkeys live a very long time, Yuba. How many dead donkeys have you seen in your life?"

"None. They don't have donkeys in Japan," I told him.

The United States is a land of variety. The people who make up that country are far more diverse than those found in Japan. There are people of all races and ethnicities—even donkeys. Even with a xenophobic president, America didn't stand to be lectured by the prime minister of Japan about its policies in that regard.

I thought there was no future for a Japan tied down by its own rules and unable to escape its long recession, which was why I had crossed the Pacific to come here. But I was getting nowhere with my actual research, and I developed a complex about my English ability. The only thing I was doing well was turning hyper-local features of Japan into science fiction novels. No matter how far I traveled, there was a sense of locale that had seeped into my being that could not be washed away.

A while later, Dr. Kawasaki sent me a bill for his services. Unsurprisingly, the use of the structural genetic field canceler was not covered by my health insurance.

"Mmmm," I grumbled, tilting my head to the right as I pondered this quandary. Fortunately, my full range of motion had returned. Then I looked at the royalty check that Kadokawa sent me for my book.

"Mmmm," I grumbled, tilting my head to the left.

(This afterword is a work of fiction.)